MAROON LAND

2

Dedication

I would like to dedicate this project to two people to whom I hold in high esteem.

First and foremost I would like to thank Chaplain Preston Jones for being my mentor who gives me daily guidance and providing me with the spiritual motivation that keeps me striving. His guidance is increasingly important as I attempt to strengthen my faith in the Lord Jesus Christ.

I'd also like to dedicate this novel to Mr. Melvin Wrenn who has always taken more than the allotted time to share his experiences, a good laugh and the way to move forward in strengthening my relationship and faith in Jesus Christ.

Thank you both for your time, support and dedication to my spiritual growth as well as helping me to be a better Christian and a better man.

Maroons

Descendants of Africans in the Americas who formed settlements away from slavery. Some had escaped from slavery on plantations to form independent communities, but others had always been free, including those born in such settlements.

Chapter 1

The swamps went from being a natural boundary where even a good man with any type of salt refrained from risking life or limb for the sake of a few dollars for a passel of escaped slaves. For most if not all of it just wasn't worth it. Colonel Thornton Davis was a different kind of Cracker though.

"Willie Maude. You know Willie Maude. She sayed the colonel got half da po' white trash in Savannah and Charleston all likkered up and ready to ride. Say he payin' dem boys a dolla' a day and fo' dat kind of money dem boys will ride day and night", Sister Anne stated matter-of-factly.

"I know dat's right. Dey was a sorry befo' lot but afta General Sherman come a callin' dey jes downright pathetic." Ruth rumbled emitting a laugh. "Truthfully speaking though, I ain't seen too many look as bad as dey do right through here. Lotta dem peckerwoods is on da brink a starvin' ta death," Ruth added tapping the corn cob pipe on the ground before digging into her pouch for some fresh tobacco.

A tall stately gentleman of ebony complexion and darker than midnight had a seat on the log next to Ruth. Taking the pipe from her hand and digging into his own leather pouch he filled it before handing it back to the old woman.

"Any word on the colonel, Thomas?"

"Not really. He came as he said would with about a hundred or so men. Half of them are so drunk they're having a hard time just staying on their mounts. I don't know how many fell off their mounts when the first shots rang out. We hit them before they hit the swamps, then baited them in. They lost a few more to the bogs and quicksand. I guess you could say they're in over their heads auntie," Thomas said grinning broadly.

"And they always will be. They'll always fail as long as they believe in superiority and—how do dey say it—entitlement dat's supposed to make 'em betta than us. White man's ego will be his downfall. You jes wait and see."

"Preach sista preach," Sister Anne said raising and shaking both hands in jubilation.

"You right auntie." Thomas concluded. "They really do believe we're inferior. They bring a hundred men when we number ten thousand men of fighting age. Ten thousand well trained troops."

"And how many of our women folk fought in our last battle against them Tennessee Volunteers?"

"You're right auntie. And they led the skirmish tonight and fought well tonight as well."

"I guess when we saw the colonel and his army we was jes s'pozed ta fall adown and thank him for taking our freedom away again and puttin' us in shackles."

"And ya know da colonel will run ta da governor afta this latest outrage."

"And say what? That he led an unprovoked attack on some unknowing slaves in the swamps and was rebuked by nature. It was not our aim to bring harm, injury or death to our attackers but only to dissuade them from doing us any harm."

"And I know you ain't so naïve as to b'lieve dat dat's how da colonel will relay what happened here tonight."

"It would be prudent if he did. If father had given the order we could have wiped them out easily," Thomas stated.

"With people like da colonel in charge the South doesn't stand a chance in da upcoming war," the stout woman known as

Sister Anne said gently pulling on her pipe. "Dey tell me South Carolina has already seceded."

"You're right again auntie. The man has no concept of military strategy. Like you said the man's running on pure ego and a sense of entitlement."

"And Lawd knows dat's a shonuff recipe to meet an early grave."

"Just hope it doesn't come at our expense," the tall young man with the chiseled frame said before standing and grabbing the reigns to the pretty sorrel grazing on the dandelions that grow so plentiful.

"Good night auntie, Miss Ann.

Chapter 2

Thomas rode back to the front as though it were any other night. The air was cool with a whisper of the cold winter that lay ahead. But tonight all was right with the world.

By all accounts he was in his twentieth fall, had been well educated by those around him who had all ascended on the colony from various parts of life but all for the same dynamic, freedom.

Thomas was a bright, young, man who learned to listen and imbibe off the riches presented to him by those his parents deemed valuable to his overall growth.

Everyone that came into contact with him said that he was his father's son, both handsome and charming but too often he found himself at odds with his own spontaneity and reckless abandon. It was this same reckless abandon that led to his own mother's demise three years earlier.

Folks christened her a saint, a martyr but both he and his father knew that if she could have only had the discipline to harness her hatred for those same Southern planters who had both enslaved and killed her father she may have still been among them but there had been, could be no remorse, nor mercy on her part.

Blinded by her own bitter hatred she'd led her elite squad of eight women into a well-planned ambush. He nor his father had ever spoken about this after her death but they both knew the truth.

All was quiet now as Thomas trotted back to where there had been gunfire. After twenty years living in Maroon he had grown not to trust the quiet. Making his way past the rear guard he quickly found his father dug in in his usual foxhole.

"How's it looking papa?"

"I think that little foray by your ladies sobered 'em up a bit," the old man chuckled. "They've been quiet for some time now but Tanya sent word that they haven't made any attempts to leave. I've sent for the mayor and the sheriff. They're both aware that we're here, don't bother or cause trouble or harm to anyone. They also know that we will defend ourselves. They're both good men so I'll let them address the colonel and his men."

Thomas heard and didn't hear his father. His thoughts were interrupted when papa mentioned 'the girls'. Now he was almost sorry he'd trained the women who in more instances than not were the first ones in, even if they were basically a sniper unit and were at a distance. Since mama's death he'd begun to have second thoughts. And now with Tanya leading the brigade he had even more trepidations

Lifelong friends, mama had taken her in when Massa Brent sold off her mother and older brother. She couldn't have been more than seven or eight at the time. The two had grown up together. A year younger than he, the two competed for everything and on any given day Tanya could hold her own and it was common knowledge that she was the best shot in Maroon with both rifle and handgun.

And then one day she suddenly took on the characteristics of a woman and woke up all the fellows who'd previously laid dormant. Even Thomas went from being childhood friend and rival to big brother and protector. So good was he in his new role that not a suitor of all those that attempted to court her was able to make any headway before he dismissed them. Tanya fed up with Thomas in his new role accused him of being overprotective.

"These Negroes don't want you T. they don't want no more than to be the first to know your forbidden."

"But Thomas what you fail to realize is they can only do or go as far as I allow them to go."

Thomas may have heard her but ignored her remarks.

"And you know brothers like Jeremiah gonna keep sniffin' around until you get weak and the rest is history."

16

"It's funny that you bring up Jeremiah. He is kind of cute you know. If there's anyone I would consider letting get close to my—how do you put it—oh yeah, my forbidden it would probably be Jeremiah.. He is awfully cute you know?" Tanya said smiling at the grimacing Thomas before getting up and walking away.

It was on this day only weeks ago when Thomas came to realize that that this woman, his lifelong friend, would never, could never belong to anyone else but him. Only now was not the time.

Papa, was the founder of the ever-growing colony. He acted as both the president and in war time situations, the general and had been since its inception. The role never appeared to be much. Of course, it had been a lot easier when mama was alive with her shouldering much of the weight of the growing colony. Now and with mama gone Thomas just accepted her duties along with his own. Now there was hardly a moment for himself.

"I'm gonna make my rounds papa."

17

"You do that son and tell Tanya she did a fine job at holding the colonel and his men at bay," his father said smiling.

Thomas made his way out of the two man foxhole, mounted the chestnut sorrel and made his way along the outskirts of the perimeter until he heard a woman's voice in the underbrush.

"Who goes there?"

"It's me. Thomas," he said knowing that he was in the sights of a Winchester. One wrong move and he was a goner. Seconds later, a slim figure moved from the thicket.

"Oh, hey Thomas," the pretty, petite, young woman said lowering the rifle.

"Hey Crystal. How are things looking?"

"Everything's quiet." The young woman said pointing to the valley in the distance before handing Thomas her binoculars.

Glancing in the distance, Thomas made out the colonel who stood in the midst of his men in full battle regalia.

"Trying to organize some type of attack I gather," Thomas remarked.

"Some men just can't accept defeat."

"No, unfortunately they can't. Tell the women to be ready but not to fire unless fired upon. We don't want to be seen as being the aggressor. Sheriff should be here soon. We'd much rather he diffuse the situation. Legal like you know," Thomas mused.

"I gotcha. I'll spread the word," Crystal smiled taking in all of Thomas while Thomas only hoped that Tanya would be as receptive although he seriously doubted that she would be.

Riding past a few of his trainees he nodded cordially until he reached Tanya who was barking orders to her charges.

"We'll give them a few more minutes to regroup and then we'll lead them back into the swamps. Only this time we'll wait until they're in the bogs and quicksand and then we'll fire making their escape damn near impossible. I expect we can knock them all out if we pull this off. I want my sharpshooters on the edge of the perimeter. Make sure your shots ring true ladies. Wait for my command."

Thomas said nothing but waited for the ladies to disperse.

"Hey T.," Thomas said relieved to find her unharmed and jovial despite the impending danger. "Papa wants you to know that you did a fine job."

"Tell papa I said thanks but our work isn't done here yet. I know papa didn't send you out here just to tell me that though. Are you out here just to check on me Thomas?"

Thomas had to smile.

"No, but seriously Tanya papa needs you to wait until the sheriff has a chance to talk to the colonel and his men."

"Oh, c'mon Thomas you and I both know that these fools ain't goin' nowhere. These here are sportin' men and their idea of fun is to tar and featherin' as many niggas as they can lay their hands on."

"I don't doubt that you're right T. but papa thinks it's important that the authorities know who the provocateurs are."

"Okay. If those are papa's wishes then so be it. Now about you. What are you up to besides stalking young women like myself?' She said winking at the now embarrassed young man standing before her.

"You know what I don't understand about you T.? We slept under the same roof until mama died and I always looked out and took up for you. But what I never understood is why you couldn't be satisfied with being a seamstress or a teacher and

21

especially after watching mama doing the same thing you're doing now. I just don't get it. Help me to understand. Do you have a death wish? You know how much I care about my people and especially for those closest to me who risk their lives simply for the thrill killing gives them."

"Listen Thomas, I don't want to argue with you but I do appreciate the concern," Tanya said brushing up against him. "We'll wait until we hear from you until we make a move," Tanya said standing on her tippy toes and giving him a peck on the cheek. "Good luck baby," she smiled before throwing the Winchester over her shoulder. It was a losing cause Thomas thought.

"Same to you and be careful T. Gotta go. Gotta make the rounds," Thomas said swinging up onto the chestnut and heading back to his father wondering if he'd ever understand women or himself for that matter.

Mama had raised Tanya and Lord knows she'd picked up all of mama's passions and other nuances and he loved them all except her desire for battle, warfare and killing. She like mama was not of this world, this America, this peculiar institution and like mama she was out to eradicate all the injustices she felt had to be endured by her people.

Like mama she seemed resigned to exterminate the lynchings, the rapes and all else that were common to slavery. Mama had long ago resigned herself to the fact that she would give her life before ever being subjected to servitude again.

Tanya had listened to mama rant and rave about the atrocities she'd seen and witnessed and prescribed to the very same doctrine and being that mama was her idol she picked up the gauntlet and fought with the same passion and reckless abandon that mama fought with outdueling the best of the Maroon soldiers in one event or another.

23

So good had she become that Thomas forbade her from competing against his men to keep his men's morale intact. Deep down he was elated inside when she won but this was different. This was real. The colonel and his men were intent on maiming and killing   just because. There was really no reason for his premeditated genocide and for some unknown reason Tanya was intent on making herself the primary target.

"If we want white people to respect us we've got to hold our heads high, fight and take what's rightfully ours. We can't drop our heads, shuffle and cow tow to their crazy-ass demands. It's our hard work and toil that built this nation. Now it's time for us to take what is rightfully ours. You know mama would have told you the same thing."

Thomas knew that mama couldn't have expressed it any clearer or said it any better. And for the first time Thomas considered what kind of man his father truly was as Tanya's words rang out in his ears. Thomas made his way back to his father who was now in the company of both the mayor and the sheriff.

"I can only say that I wish all of my constituents were as logical and sensible as you are Papa," Mayor Allen said shaking papa's hand.

"If they were there would be no need for a mayor or sheriff to mediate disputes such as these," Sheriff Body smiled. "Knuckleheads like these keep us employed. I'll speak to them on the way out but in all honesty I don't think it's going to do any good. Half of 'em left town drunk and there was no talking to them then and I don't think much has changed since then.

Give me about a half an hour to get clear of them and then do what you have to do Mr. Man. I understand your need to protect you and yours but please get rid of the bodies when it's over. They'll be wives and children looking to find out what

25

happened to their loved ones and we don't want this to blossom into anything bigger than it already is.

It would be nice if they would turn around and go home of their own accord but like I said if they choose otherwise and anyone gets a whiff about what really happened I will attest to the fact that you were doing no more than defending yourselves. And like the mayor said, thanks for the heads up. Just a shame these men don't know what they're up against," the sheriff said before shaking papa's hand and riding off.

An hour later a rider came into camp.

"They sent some riders downstream and a few upstream. Ms. Tanya said she thinks they're probably trying to either flank us or find an easier way to get around the swamps. Another twenty or so more men rode in and it looks like they're ready to mount a charge suh."

"Good job Tracy," papa said. "Tell Tanya to have the women pick off anyone who raises their head or comes out in the open."

"Yas, suh," the pretty, young woman turned, riding off the same way she came.

"Thomas, I want you to circle around and hit them from the rear as soon as we hit them from the front. Cut off the road. As soon as they turn we'll catch them in the crossfire. Make sure your people stay high or stay low so they don't get caught in the crossfire."

"I gotcha papa."

Thomas dug into his foxhole and dozed off. Dante, his boyhood friend and second in command lay awake on guard.

"Party's starting Man," he said shaking Thomas. The snap and pop of rifle fire brought Thomas Man to his senses. Grabbing his hat he mashed it down on his baldhead desperately trying to

27

find out where the shots were coming from. It was quickly apparent that the sheriff's words had fallen on deaf ears.

"Gear up men! Look alive! Take your time and make each shot count! Don't rush! No need to panic! We've been here before!" Papa shouted at the men under his command.

Thomas controlled the cavalry but it had already been decided that they were hardly needed in protecting their defensive stronghold which was surrounded by swamps filled with copperheads, gators and every type of poisonous reptile imaginable.

Papa had obviously given the order. Mounting his horse quickly Thomas set out in the direction of the first shots with ten of his most trusted men at his heels. No order had been given. He was their commanding officer and friend and when he mounted up at the sound of gunfire they did so as well. Dante was already there when he arrived.

"What's good D.?"

"It's all good. Tanya's team hit 'em hard causing them to scatter. She's got 'em pinned down and her snipers are picking them off one-by-one any time they show their faces. If papa would hit 'em hard from the front this could be over in less than an hour."

"Our men have the rear locked up?"

"Locked up and down."

"Good. Well let's get up there so we can get a better picture," Thomas said turning and riding off towards the sound of more gunfire from the road.

Chapter 3

Confused and slightly worried, Tanya had to know how
Thomas Man felt about her. She had to know that he loved her and
had plans for her but she refused to listen or take heed when it
came to her fighting for her principles. And once more he found
himself calling on his God to protect her and preventing any harm
from coming to her.

Ten minutes later he found her once again barking orders to
her troops.

"I need someone over there in the trees. I don't want any
places, any field of fire left open where they can slip through and
escape. Is that understood ladies? This is like a turkey shoot
ladies." Three women all who appeared older nodded and made
their way into the underbrush.

"How you doin' T.?"

"Was expectin' a bit more from this highly decorated colonel but I'm really not seeing anything to impress me. Nothin' more than a shepherd leading his sheep to slaughter. I mean I see nothing in the way of a plan or strategy. No scouting, no surveillance, no plan whatsoever. This isn't even challenging," the disappointment obvious in her voice.

I don't think you and the colonel are on the same wavelength T. He sees little or no need for military strategy or any other plan for that matter. All he needs to know is that he's carrying out his strategy."

"And what is his strategy?"

"To round up a bunch of ignorant, heathen, law-breaking niggas and return them to their rightful owners for a fairly handsome reward. You know a good, strong, buck will bring anywhere from a thousand to fifteen hundred dollars easily. I can almost guarantee that he never considered armed resistance from a bunch of Colored runaway slaves. To begin with niggas ain't smart enough to organize let alone to come together and put up any kind of resistance.

If he lives to tell about this we'll get quite a different kind of story of how today's skirmish transpired. The way he'll tell it will be how an army of close to a thousand well-armed, well trained Colored runaway slaves attacked his band of a hundred men. His men fought with much valor and courage but were both outgunned and out manned. He was lucky to have escaped with his life."

"In that case, he mustn't be allowed to escape," Tanya replied staring at the ground in front of her.

"Do what you have to do. Just promise me you'll bring home everyone safely," Thomas said knowing that his command now made him responsible for the carnage and killing that was about to take place. Of one thing he was sure that this woman would delight in the bloodletting about to take place and that the alligators would eat well for weeks to come.

"Thomas."

"Yes, T."

"If your men could just skirt the perimeter and draw them out it would make my ladies job a lot quicker and a lot easier."

"I wish I could help you T. But I can't afford to put my men in that kind of danger. What you're asking would put my men in harm's way and you know me well enough to know that I would never do that. You volunteered for this detail and from what I can see this looks like a war of attrition.

They should come crawling out of their holes within a week's time in hopes of mercy, half-starved and dying of thirst. They'll probably run out of food and water. And I don't envy them white flag in hand begging for mercy. As you know there is to be no quarter and no mercy which means cold blooded murder. I'm sorry but this is a burden that you alone must carry."

"Whether you realize it or not I feel no burden or distress carrying this weight I know these same men would have no problem carrying out a similar order if the tables were turned. These same type men with the same mind set had no problem when they killed my mother. Trust me I won't have the slightest problem putting an end to their wretched lives."

"I hear you T. But remember never to let your hatred make you bitter. If you do it will consume you and eat you alive." He said glancing at the pretty young woman with the buckskin, dress that hugged her long, thick, chocolate thighs just the way Thomas wanted to.

Dante rode up as Thomas and Tanya stared deeply in each other's eyes.

"I don't know why you two don't just cut through the chase and all the melodrama and just go on and get hitched." Tanya dropped her head blushing deeply. "I ain't never seen two people more destined to tie the knot. What seems to be the hold up?"

"Stop by the house when you get through with this," Thomas said continuing to stare at Tanya ignoring Dante almost completely.

"I'll do that," Tanya said managing a quick smile.

Thomas rode back passing Papa's troops who were now fully engaged. A steady staccato of rifle fire rang out but after the initial burst the sounds of gunfire dissipated into a shot every five or ten minutes.

"I could've told you that there would be no war of attrition if Tanya was in anyway involved. That there gals got a mean streak like I've never known. I don't know what white man ever did anything to her but they sho nuff picked the wrong gal to get on the wrong side of. You wasted your words when you said 'no quarter, no mercy'. Them there boys don't know it but they signed their death certificates when they attacked us." Dante added.

Later that night, Thomas awoke from a restless sleep and made his way to the front window. He was relieved to find a candle burning in Tanya's cabin across the square.

Papa made it a point to keep those in his inner most circle closest to him and since it didn't look right after mother's death for Tanya to be living with two men she was in no way related to. (Even if the two men were Thomas and papa). So, before anyone could say anything papa had a cabin built for T. It was too late to be knocking. Any questions he had would just have to wait until the morning.

Thomas continued to toss and turn. When he finally fell asleep it was Ms. Henry's rooster that awoke him. When he finally did awake he found Papa on the front porch with the sheriff.

"Folks are asking questions papa. Seems loved ones are missing. I'm just hoped you disposed of the bodies. papa."

Papa was smart enough to know that even with the sheriff being a friend that if he answered the question he would be implicating himself and Papa trusted no man to that extent. 'Self-preservation is the first law of nature.' Was a point he tried to drive home with me at every turn. So, he said nothing. When the sheriff was out of sight he turned to his son and protégé and simply asked.

"Were the bodies disposed of properly son?"

"I was probably in bed before you were papa. I left Tanya to handle that."

There was a quiet pause before the older man spoke.

"Never depend on anyone else. If you do it then you can take pride in the fact that you did the job and you did it well. Please speak to T. and make sure those bodies were properly disposed of. We don't need any more trouble than we already have. When you finish with her send her to me or better yet run and fetch her so we'll all be on the same page."

"Yes, father," Thomas said grabbing his favorite gray, woolen hat. Mother had made it for him not long before her death and he cherished it. Thomas made his way across the muddy street before climbing the three or four wooden steps that led to her front door. Before he could knock the door opened. Standing before him he saw his best friend, mama, and his newly crowned queen all rolled into one. In his mind she would soon be his wife and he wondered if it were possible to love her any more than he did right now.

"Good morning my handsome beau."

"Morning T. You certainly seem chipper this morning," Thomas noted smiling.

"And why shouldn't I be?" she asked cheerfully. "God has blessed me and given me another day. Do you realize how many people didn't receive that blessing this morning and won't see the light of day today." Tanya grinned. But Thomas' mind was elsewhere. How could someone so beautiful have such an obsession for fighting, for killing?

'Speaking of," Thomas whispered. "Did you dispose of those bodies?"

"C'mon Thomas. That's one of the first things we learn. You know papa considers that paramount. Get rid of the evidence. Besides you know I'm thorough. Why would you even question me?"

"I'm sorry T. It's just that the sheriff stopped by this morning to see papa. Seems some of those men's kinfolks have been lookin' for them and papa asked me the same thing. He asked me if I disposed of the bodies and I didn't have an answer. I didn't know what to say. Guess, I do now. Anyway papa wants to see us both now."

"Lead the way my knight in shining armor," Tanya said still grinning and grabbing the young man's arm.

"Morning papa," Tanya yelled grabbing and hugging the only father she'd ever known.

"You're such a sweet child," the old man grinned his fondness for the young woman obvious. "You always have been but now tell me how last night's events ended."

A somber look came to Tanya's face.

"There's really not much to tell papa. The sheriff gave them the opportunity to walk away but they decided to put up a fight, if you wanna call it that. Wasn't even a fight if you ask me? What they did was to simply sacrifice their lives.

I suppose they had ambitions of attacking a defenseless people with the hopes of selling them into the living hell that is slavery. All I can say is that group that tried last night won't have the opportunity to try that again."

"Now let me ask you this. Did you properly dispose of the bodies?"

"Papa! Not you too. Give me some credit. I was taught by two of the most knowledgeable people I know and I was well schooled in the fact that disposing of the bodies is as much a part of the battle as the actual fighting. You both taught me. Mama taught me."

Papa dropped his head. He was a bit embarrassed but couldn't help but smile. There were only a few people who could penetrate the man's stern exterior. T. was one of them and it was obvious he had a soft spot for his adopted daughter. Oh, how she reminded him of his late wife. God bless her soul.

42

T. was the daughter he never had and he the father she so longed for. A stern disciplinarian she would soon learn after being adopted into the family that this consisted of a ton of work and an immense amount of studying. There wasn't much else. Papa treated the whole village more or less like this and there were times she wondered why someone, anyone didn't just walk up to him and club him to death and put everyone out of their misery. But now that she was older she was grateful for his tactics. Now she understood.

Yet, when she was growing up she sometimes just wanted to scream, stop, as loudly as she could. Now she understood that he and mama weren't interested in molding better individuals. Instead they were building, creating the future leaders of Maroon. They knew that they weren't going to live forever so they spent every waking hour grooming the two to be their heirs.

Neither had disappointed but like all children they often seemed undisciplined and unfocused to papa. Perhaps he was demanding too much from them. After all they were still children. He remembered his wife pulling him to the side on more than one occasion telling him he was driving them too hard and pleading with him to ease up.

But deep down he liked the two and was warmed by the adults they'd become. And though both were headstrong and a bit rebellious at times he had to admit that the girl he'd adopted was bright, with leadership qualities he'd known in only one other woman, his May. And Thomas was as good a man as he'd ever come to know. Together the two would lead his flock out of Egypt and into the Promised Land. Of this he was sure.

"Did either of you think to leave a perimeter guard?"

"Yes papa. You worry too much. There's a perimeter guard as well as scouts staggered along the road. I seriously doubt

44

that we'll see or hear anything from them anytime soon though. Most of those men who attacked us last night appeared to be farmers out for a little mischief and mayhem and an extra buck or two and from what I gather their families will be hard-pressed to gather in their crops and will be occupied much of the winter just trying to get through without their men at home so I doubt if we'll see any repercussions until next spring."

"I'm in total agreement with T. papa and with the way we've been growing I don't believe we can remain here much longer. Roman Nose said he would assure us safe passage west through Indian Territory and we need land. With the new Homesteading Act we can acquire enough land west of the Mississippi say in Kansas or Missouri which aren't slave states. Perhaps we can get a fresh start with less hostility. There's even a chance we may be able to live without a constant threat and fear."

The old man had to smile.

"A panacea? Paradise huh?"

Was he laughing at them the way he used to when they were children coming up with lame brain ideas? They glanced at each other in obvious discomfort. And then he spoke.

"I do believe I've chosen the right two to lead Maroon into the next phase if not the next century. You two seem to have given this as much thought as I have. I like your reasoning and your logic is sound and I think this is as good a place as ever to begin the transition."

"The transition?" Thomas heard himself say.

"Yes, son. I've spent the last twenty-eight years preparing you two for this day."

"And what is it that you've prepared us for papa?" Tee asked inquisitively.

Papa moved to his favorite rocker, sat and pulled out his favorite corn cob pipe, filled it and inhaled deeply.

"Have a seat," he said pointing to the two wooden chairs that adorned the tiny room. Over the last twenty-eight years I've spent my time trying to build a viable community for my brothers and sisters where they could control their own destinies as free men and women of color. I would like to think I helped to give them a chance to rebuild their lives. Now I think it's time for an old man to relinquish those duties and who better to carry on that dream than my heirs."

"You're not serious papa?" T. interjected.

"Believe me. He's serious. Papa's tired." Thomas said directing his attention to Tanya.

"I ran away from the McCaffrey place twenty-eight years ago with your mother and six others. In all there were eight of us and back then things were entirely different. Talk about tough

47

times. We didn't have clothes or food but we endured. In that first year we were never in any one place for more than a week and the blood hounds were always nipping at our hills.

Some nights we slept in trees. Other nights we had to stay in the water all night with trees hanging over to just to hide our scent but we never gave up hope and we persevered. Those were tough times and often I felt like throwing the towel in and just giving up but May refused to let me, God bless her soul. She was a fighter. No, there was no quit in her. She kept me going until we came upon this place.

Now they tell me that at last count we numbered somewhere around twenty thousand. Many of those that find us have no idea what they are coming to or where they are going. What they do know is that anything is better than that white man wielding that whip and shackles. My job Has always been to give them protection and some purpose for their lives. We give them a purpose for living in a relatively peaceful community. Most, if not all of the drama comes from without and as you know our young men and women are adamant about maintaining their freedom and train extremely hard so as not to be taken and are willing to risk their lives to stay free. And that is primarily why we stay victorious. A man can fight for money and material gains but he can never win against a man fighting for his life. That is why we cannot be defeated by forces equal in number. The reason is because we have purpose. We are fighting for our lives.

It is our job to instill this training, faith and belief in themselves. This is our job. We must teach them. Give them pride and a purpose for living. Your mother and I did that but a council of your elders may be helpful in guiding you and helping you govern such a large body. And trust me you are about to see a doubling or even a tripling of growth now that war is on the horizon.

You may also consider delegating many of the duties your mother and I just took for granted. What I would suggest is that you set up committees to handle much of the hard work. Just make sure you pay them fairly."

"And just where do you propose we get the money to pay these people papa?"

"Thomas?" the old man said turning to his son.

"We will have to propose taxes or a tariff," Thomas elicited.

"Oh okay. I see you too have discussed this already."

"Not really. We just threw around a couple of ideas like how we were going to continually outfit the army," papa said.

"And how can we do that and what will we tax?" T. asked.

"For now we can tax the fact that we offer protection and that army must be paid as well as the need for arms. In essence we are giving the people refuge from those intent on harming or enslaving them." Thomas said.

"From what I see in listening to you two is that more than anything you two may need to present a unified front. You cannot lead if you are at odds over everything. And don't get the wrong idea. It's not that I'm trying to rush you into anything but when you come before the people you must come as one.

Although there are two of you and you are individuals when you address the populace you must come as one unified front. You must stand together. You've gotta be unified in your beliefs. The unified front your mother and I presented did us a world of good. It made us not only more formidable but our love for each other showed the community that we were focused and creditable."

T. dropped her head. A grin a mile wide spread across her face. Thomas sat there at a complete loss for words. When the other fellows his age were building their own huts mama had suddenly been killed and there was no way he could leave his father alone. Now he was being burdened with the responsibility of caring for twenty-thousand lost souls but if this was papa's requests then so be it but the idea of his having to marry to present a united front was simply more than he could bear. In the back of his mind he had all intention of making T. his wife but in his own time.

Still, he couldn't argue with the mate chosen for him. After all, it was inevitable. But what really bothered him was the choice being made for him and the fact that his marriage was no longer a choice but a requirement for a job he was not all that sure he wanted.

Tanya, on the other hand, was elated and fit to be tied. Beside herself the only thing she wondered about now was how Thomas would approach her. She liked the fact that papa had put him on the spot and no matter what he felt she knew he would never question papa's wishes.

She wouldn't have to wait long for her answer as later that evening he stopped by the council as was his daily ritual and waited for her as she bridled her horse. Wearing his favorite tan deerskin dress she looked especially ravishing. Together they rode to the front gate in silence. Not a single word passed between them and slightly disappointed T. rode on to check on her squad.

"What's good D.?"

"I'm not exactly sure Thomas. There seems to be some movement out there most of the night but the scouts aren't able to really make out anything as there are no fires. The girls and the scouts are all reporting the same thing but I can't really get a fix on how many there are or what they're intent is. I can't tell if they're Rebs or runaways."

Dante handed his friend the spyglass but Thomas could see

53

A minute or so later, Tanya rode in.

"My girls are telling me there's a whole lotta movement but they can't seem to make out who it is or what they're doing."

"Send a squad and tell them to get in as close as they can and see what's going on. In the meantime, double the guard. But let's see what it is they're after before they get a chance to cross the swamps."

"I already did. Sent some of your men. I let papa know and sent for the rest of my ladies."

Thomas was forced to smile. He wanted to kick himself. Papa had actually made it easy on him. He would never have had the courage to ask for her hand, not at this time anyway. But now that it was out in the open he took her hand in his and led her away from Dante and his men.

"I think papa's right and I think I've been putting this off for far too long but I'd be honored if you'd be my wife Tanya."

54

Tanya smiled knowing she had him she stuck out her hand indicating there was no ring.

"Oh my goodness. I guess I got so caught up in the idea that I just didn't think…"

"Just? I've known you were going to be my husband since we were kids. I know papa's mentioning it wasn't the first time it came to you? Men," Tanya sighed deeply.

Thomas leaned over to kiss his fiancée when at least twenty rode in.

"Where you want us T.?"

"Same places as usual. And have a couple of girls get close enough to keep an eye on them and see what they're up to. Keep me posted. I'll be right behind you. And be safe."

Turning back to Thomas she smiled.

"You were saying." No sooner had the words escaped her lips than more soldiers rode up.

"Where you want us boss?"

"Mix in with Dante's men. Move half the squad up within rifle distance just in case."

"Gotcha."

"Guess this just isn't the right time or place," Tanya said mounting the brown and white appaloosa. "I'll talk to you later, husband to be," she said showing al of her pearly whites.

"Damn it." He murmured under his breath.

Climbing into the foxhole next to Dante Thomas cursed again. How long he had waited for his lips to touch hers and he was so close and yet he would still have to wait.

"What's wrong Man?"

"Papa assigned me to be his successor tonight."

"And you're fussin'. I mean c'mon. We both knew that was comin'. So, what's the problem? I kinda figured you'd be overjoyed. You must know that papa has to be exhausted especially the way Maroon has grown."

"True and in my new capacity I'd like to assign you control of both men's and women's armies. And I want to make it a requirement that every male that hits the age of sixteen that it's mandatory that he enlist and serve two years."

Dante smiled broadly.

"That's all well and good my friend but you fail to realize that I already have a small army of my own at home that rely on me to train them as well."

"Which is one of the reasons I chose you to lead these men. Our whole existence as a maroon colony depends on us being able to defend ourselves against outsiders and you and Dido know military warfare and strategy better than anyone in the colony and the men have a certain rapport with you that they don't have with Dido making you the perfect candidate."

"You already know I'm going to have to run this by Helen before I can accept your offer and being commander-in-chief of an armed forces is a full time job and I do have a family to provide for you know."

"All that's been taken into consideration and you will be fully compensated. I assure you and yours will be handsomely rewarded."

"I see you've crossed all the 'i's' and dotted all the 't's'."

"Yes. C'mon Dante you don't make rash decisions which is why I know running this army is a piece of cake for you. I watch you and your men and I know that if you asked them they would walk through a wall of fire for you. That's why I know you'd be a great leader. But don't rush your decision. Think some time to think about it. One thing I do know is that you'd be much better giving orders than taking them. So, take your time and think about it." Thomas grinned. "I need an answer by morning."

No sooner had he finished than a rider rode in.

"There are about sixty or seventy riders in all, some in Confederate uniforms. Every five or ten minutes, another ten or fifteen ride in. Suh, if I may share my opinion…" the young man said.

"Go ahead Corporal Brent."

"I'm thinkin' we may wanna hit 'em before they turn into a full-fledged army is all suh."

"You may be right. Thanks for the suggestion corporal."

And with that said Corporal Brent turned and rode back to his post.

"He could be very well be right ya know," Dante mused.

"The way cotton has taken over we're worth far too much right through here and we pose a significant threat. With our numbers we could ride against anybody and to be honest I like our chances."

"It's your call. You're in charge now. So, what do you propose general?"

"I thought you were giving me some time to think about it?"

"I reconsidered. I need you by my side. I'm gonna need my right hand man."

By the time Thomas was finished directing his men Tanya was back in the saddle.

"You're riding off without me?" he asked

"We have a lifetime hon."

Chapter 4

Sliding back into the foxhole next to Dante his friend looked at Thomas and soon knew what was troubling Thomas.

Dante's wife Helen and the mother of his six children was one of the first to join mama when she was looking for enlistees for her all women's sniper brigade. Dante could only smile. He'd known Thomas Man all of his life and although they were virtually inseparable there were a few things that his friend chose not to share. And yet he didn't have to. Dante could read him like a book. This time was no different as he lay there waiting for Thomas to speak on what it was that was troubling him.

"Dante tell me something?"

"What up Man?" he said trying his best to cover the grin he knew was there.

"How do you not worry when Helen's out there in the midst of the mix when men are out there taking careful aim and trying their able bodied best to kill her?"

This was not the line of questioning Dante was expecting and had to sit back and think long and hard.

"I have long ago come to accept the fact that I can only control certain things in my life. The rest I have to put in the Good Lord's hands. Let me ask you this Thomas. Why do you risk your life to come out here and battle men you have never met? Whatever your reason it is enough to have you risk your life. Whatever Helen's reason is it means enough for her to come out and risk hers. I have to respect that. We have all felt the effects, the brunt of this evil institution. Like I said you have to respect their reasons for fighting it and put the rest in God's hands. You're just lucky you're not married. The worry only gets worse when you tie the knot"

"Thanks. Just what I needed to hear. You know I proposed to T. tonight."

"Well, I'll be goddamned! It's about time. Congratulations my brother," Dante said grabbing and hugging Thomas and letting everyone within earshot know their position. "Didn't I tell you two were destined? I've never met two people who care about each other the way you two do. It was meant to be. I'm happy for you my brother! I really am happy for you."

An hour an hour later Dante made his way out of the foxhole and made his way towards his men. Hearing horses in the distance he knew Dante had sent a messenger to tell the girls. Soon a runner could be heard coming in their direction. Thomas met the messenger before returning to his men.

"We're moving up to attack. Fire when you have a target in range.

Take careful aim and make sure your shots count. The women will engage them first. We'll move up under the cover of their fire."

Not fifteen minutes later the men were settled into position on a sharp cliff overlooking the dismal swamp below where it seemed as if men were coming in by the droves.

Seems the word had come in that a statewide recruiting campaign had been placed in every nook and cranny of the state seeking any and all that were intent on keeping the Southern way of life alive in these troubled times. The ad went on to claim that a large band of renegade niggas intent on attacking Southern planters was responsible for the massacre of Colonel Thornton Davis and his entire army of men whose only intent was to disband the slaves. These renegade slaves had ambushed the colonel and his men, driven them into the swamps and either shot them, drowned them or left them to be eaten by gators. Now was the time for action and an opportunity to put these niggas in their rightful place. All able bodied men who were interested in seeing justice done should meet at the Ol' Forks Road to put down this nigga rebellion that could wreak havoc. Across the entire South

It was a call to arms and from the size of the militia now gathered the call to arms had not been taken at all lightly. This nigga rebellion could not be taken lightly.

After an hour of observing the men below Thomas realized the scouts suggestion was probably the best alternative. Hit them hard and send them on their way. He watched as the mob below did little to hide their presence. And still more rode into camp. Thomas hated to second guess his newly appointed general but they needed to attack now before they had a chance to organize and propose a method of attack. And then as if Dante were reading his mind he heard the drums, raised his rifle to his shoulder and squeezed one off.

The ball hit the young man flush in his chest. The man who appeared no older than Thomas never knew what hit him. He left his feet and slammed into the tree three feet behind him.

At first, the men around him were more than a little startled and chaos reigned throughout the makeshift camp and then the cry rang out.

"Runaway niggas! And they're armed. 'Take cover men!" Someone shouted. And then a second order was given.

"Don't shoot to kill. A dead nigga ain't worth nothin'. Remember men. There's five hundred dollars a head on every one captured alive."

So, this is what this was all about Thomas thought before raising his rifle eye level. What they didn't know was that his people had tasted freedom and were willing to risk their very lives before relinquishing it again.

Meanwhile, Dante sent word to Tanya and Helen to cut the road off not allowing anyone to enter or exit. But there was more. Never had he seen more Southern Crackers so intent on dislodging them from their homes. But then never had so many Colored runaways amassed in one place. How many thousands dollars were the inhabitants of Maroon worth? There was more but he had to put his thoughts on hold for now. There was a battle to be won.

Two days later, Thomas made sure the bodies were buried deep in the swamp. The Southerners fought well but in the end it simply came down to them being outnumbered, out gunned and out maneuvered. Surveying the battlefield before being led to the four surviving members of the Southern entourage were now being held to await trial.

"Nigga, I will have your hide if you don't cut me loose this instant."

"Scuse me suh but I don't think you're in any position to be making demands," Dante mused.

"You obviously don't know who I am or how much weight I carry," the colonel shouted.

"I really don't give a damn who you are or how much weight you carry. What I do know is that you and your men attacked civilians and will be tried by a military tribunal for your crimes against humanity," Thomas calmly replied.

The well decorated colonel couldn't help but laugh.

"Perfect example of why you don't give niggas no education," he said turning to his fellow captives.

"You're absolutely right suh but at the moment we have more pressing matters to discuss like what gives you the right to attack innocent women and children whose only intent is to live in peace. We do not come to your door with the intent of raping and enslaving your loved ones."

68

"Nigga is you questioning me? In the proper order of things you ain't nothing but my property. You belong to me. You understand? All you niggas belong to me. It's my job to prevent insurrections just such as these nigga. God has ordained me..."

The colonel did not get a chance to finish his testimony when Thomas stood up.

"How many times have we heard similar words from white men who see no wrong in their actions? This man shows no remorse for trying to capture and enslaving us and it is by law that we hang this coward by his neck until dead for his unprovoked crimes against us. Let me see a show of hands for all in favor." Thomas proclaimed as he'd seen papa do on numerous occasions.

"I see no other alternative. As Thomas stated, this man shows no remorse and I'm afraid that if freed it would only be a matter of time before he'd gather another army. I do believe his very words sealed his verdict," Dante ventured. So, I ask you once

69

again brothers and sisters to seal the fate of these four captives. He said standing and seconding Thomas as was proper protocol.

A loud chorus of 'Ayes' was heard from all gathered and the four men were sentenced to death.

The following day, Thomas sat with his father who now acted solely as his advisor and concierge moving forward. He then called for a meeting with the elders before finally meeting with his own hand-picked council which consisted of Dante, his newly appointed general, his future wife and head of the women's auxiliary, and advisor. Dido, another of his boyhood companions and devout history buff was also commissioned to serve as an advisor. Dido had a passion for military history and the two men debated military strategy on a daily basis. An invaluable asset, Thomas always kept Dido in close proximity. But T, his future was the confidante for Thomas when he could not go to the other three knowing his most inner thoughts, his visions and his dreams for Maroon.

Nowadays the way Thomas looked at her she was convinced they would have their own army when it came to children and so a four bedroom house was a modest request and not out of the question. When one considered that Thomas now the leader, the governor, and patriarch of Maroon a four bedroom house wasn't an unreasonable request.

Tanya completed the council.

"Friends, I have spoken to everyone but you but I am here to ask for your help, your advice and your suggestions. A few things have helped me come to this decision. The first is our ever increasing numbers. We have simply outgrown the land and because of our numbers we are drawing undo and unwanted attention. In the last month alone we have been attacked three times. Each time their armies grow larger than the time before.

71

Because they don't know how strong we are they tend to underestimate our strength. That's to our advantage but when the war comes—and it is coming—I want us to be as far away from the fighting as possible.

Recently President Lincoln instituted the Homestead Act which allows us to own our own land and I think that's our best bet. I've spoken to Roman Nose and he's guaranteed us safe passage through Indian Territory so what I need from you is your thoughts, ideas and suggestions."

Dante raised his hand as if they were still in school.

"Talk to me D."

"Just wanted to know if you'd set the date yet?" He said smiling. Thomas could only drop his head to hide the widening grin spreading across his face.

"I'm planning on it just as soon as we get settled," Thomas replied matter-of-factly and was glad to see the receptiveness of his inner circle in seeking out a new home.

Almost to a person they decided that they needed to leave now as opposed to the following spring as had been proposed. It was obvious they were tired of being threatened and harassed. In the end they'd given the community two weeks to gather their harvests and say goodbye to loved ones on nearby plantations.

It was funny though. As badly as most wanted to find a new home there were more than a few families that had come to know the swamps as their home and chose to remain. Thomas made sure he saw to their needs, making sure they were well armed. In all, close to five thousand families including well over twelve thousand well-trained troops prepared to make the move.

The day of the departure was a dark, day, autumn day. A nip in the air prognosticating winter made the move from the only home many of them had ever known a painfully sad day. The unknown loomed large and there was a quiet pall over almost everyone.

Pooling community resources Thomas bought every wagon in the immediate area and after a full two weeks of preparation the wagon train was ready to depart with Dante reluctantly taking the reigns as general and military commander of the expedition.

"I don't know if I'm really up for this Thomas," he said to Thomas.

"I know exactly how you feel my brother," Thomas replied. "Let's finish this conversation when we get there though."

But for now Dante had his troops split into four shifts of more than three thousand men on duty guarding the train at any one time. They made quite a formidable force in their all black uniforms and black face masks.

"Roman Nose is here to see you," one of Thomas' elite guards said sticking his head in the doorway of the tent Thomas was using as a command post.

Thomas and the tall, handsome man known as Roman Nose had grown up together and were as close as two people could be, hunting and fishing whenever time allowed. Being the first born sons of leaders weighed heavily on them as boys and drew them even closer.

"Hello my friend," said as the two men embraced. "Little Bear tells me that you are ready to leave."

"Noon tomorrow."

"Then why are you out here instead of home on your last night?"

"Just a precautionary measure. I'd hate to be attacked and caught with our pants down on our last night here. And I'm sure there will be repercussions after that last battle. Can't be too cautious."

"I understand. Tell me. How many braves do you think you will need to escort your train?"

"I have no idea. This is your country. I'm sure you know what type of threats we will encounter better than I. From what I know I don't expect any trouble from any Indians aside from the Crow and that is only based on what you have told me. From what you and Little Bear have told me they are all aware of us passing through. It is the whites and the bandits that I fear most but with a train as large as ours they would be foolish to hit us. Still, I'd be foolish not to worry."

"Understandable. What I'll do then is wait until tomorrow to see just how large a train it is and then I can best get an idea of how to guard it. I'll make sure there are no gaps in your defenses and where there is I'll fill them. I'll also post a formidable perimeter. Your women and children will be safe. You have my word my brother."

"Sounds like a plan and I appreciate it my friend."

"I will see you in the morning. Oh, and by the way I believe congratulations are in order. Can't say I was surprised. I always knew. The only question was when."

"Dante told you?"

"Of course, misery loves company."

"I guess you're next. You're the only one that hasn't made that commitment."

"All things in time," Roman Nose countered leading his band of young warriors out onto the grasslands.

Thomas smiled. It would be a long time before the good looking young chief of the Cheyenne would seek out a wife with all the young Indian maidens at his beck and call.

As Thomas rounded up the remainder of the horses in the corral and led them to the wagons and hitched them to the back a familiar voice beckoned him..

"Thomas honey, did you remember the cows down in the lower pasture?"

"Already have them tied to Ms. Newell's team?"

"Not trying to nag or anything sweetheart. Just don't want you to get too far down the road tomorrow and say the 'd' word you're so fond of saying because you forgot something, you cutie you." Tanya teased.

"Good lookin' out lady. But what I'm more interested in knowing is why I haven't seen or heard from you in the last couple of days?"

"Just been busy with the move and all. Tryin' to help out where I can," Tanya said her gaze falling to the ground.

"C'mon T. you know I know you better than that. What's really going on?"

"Well, to be honest with you I don't like the way you've been lookin' at me since you proposed."

"And how may I ask have I been lookin' at you?"

"I can't really explain it but it's like you're much friskier than usual since I agreed to marry you."

Thomas had to chuckle.

"Okay, okay. That may not entirely be the truth. The truth is sometimes I just want you so bad that I forget to breathe. But at the same time I want to do it the right way. I want to be married and settled before lying down with you and the only way for me to do that is to keep my distance until everything's in place.

Thomas was forced to smile.

"Chances are that once we truly hit the trail you'll be far too busy to even think about lying down with me or anything else."

"To be honest I haven't thought about anything else since you proposed."

Thomas grabbed his wife-to-be and draped his six foot four frame over her.

"I love you T."

"I love you more Man," Tanya said glad that he'd accepted her confession without being judgmental.

Chapter 5

The first month proved if nothing else hard and uneventful. The wagon train which was more than three miles in length slept for no more than an hour a day.

"Move up! Keep those wagons together. If those children can't do any better than that then carry them or throw them in with one of the supply wagons." Dante shouted prodding those travelers who chose to walk after having ridden for hours.

The trail was rigid and tough especially on the older travelers and small children. The sprawling plains gave want for little and were full of wild game. Fresh meat was plentiful and in the first month Dante had drilled the loosely collected army into a well-oiled fighting machine with daily maneuvers on the run. When they weren't on guard duty they found themselves training and deploying different strategies and movements. They were if nothing else prepared and ready.

In the evenings when they stopped to rest Dido would gather the recruits who had not been on duty that day and teach them military strategy preparing Dante with his next class of military officers.

During Dante's tenure in the field with his men he somehow still found time to spend with his own children. When away his oldest Nat, a rare child, chose to spend any leisure time around his Uncle Man who the boy of fifteen idolized.

"And who's watching your family while your father's away?" Tanya said vying for the little time she had to spend with Thomas who rarely had time for her anymore.

"Papa left soldiers. If you can get past them there are Roman Nose's braves. I don't think my family has too much to worry about Auntie T."

82

Thomas was forced to smile.

"Listen Nat. You run along now. We'll talk some more tomorrow."

Standing and turning the boy left the fire dejectedly and headed back to his own wagon.

"That boy loves him some Man. He'd go to the ends of the earth for his Uncle Thomas."

"I am honored that he thinks so much of me. They tell me tomorrow we're going to cross the mighty Mississippi. Black Cloud and Little Bear tell me there's little to fear but I want you to organize it so the women and children go first after the soldiers hit the shore," Thomas mused aloud.

"Will do my husband but I have other things on my mind right now."

"Then what it is I can do for you pretty lady?"

"Nothin' other than the fact that I need to spend some time with my future husband."

"Is that it?" Thomas grinned. "That's got to be the easiest request I've had all day. Sure is better than Miss Belinda asking me to pull her heifer out of the mud. Or ol' man Lucius needing me to help lift his wagon so he can replace the axle. Talk about some back breakin' work," Thomas said grinning even more now as he looked at his beautiful fiancée, the weariness beginning to etch its mark on his furrowed brow.

Tanya was forced to laugh.

"No, no, no. It's nothing like that. Like I said I just want to spend some time with you alone is all." All the worry and stress Thomas had up until this point was suddenly gone with her words.

The night was unseasonably warm considering it was late October. Still, Tanya threw on the shawl mama had crocheted for her right before she died. Together they sat around the small fire.

She leaned into him and he took her in his arms and breathed a deep sigh of relief.

"You know the whole time I was growing up I watched papa. I idolized him. I remember one day telling papa I wanted to be just like him. And do you know what he told me?"

"No, what did he say?"

"He said be careful for what you wish for Thomas. Then he said he didn't want me to be like him. He wanted me to be better than he was."

"I know you're not doubting yourself Man."

"No, but there are times like now when I don't think I can hold a flag to what he did."

"Stop doubting yourself. There's no doubt that you can be every bit as good a leader if not better. He knows that and so do I but papa spent close to thirty years in the saddle before turning over the reins to you. You've watched but it means nothing until you're actually in the saddle.. You've only been on the job a month and from the talk it's been a fairly easy transition. At least that's the word coming back.

From what I've heard everyone seems to think you picked up right where papa left off. Everyone seems to think you're doing a fabulous job." Tanya said snugglin' up closer to her man. "What you've got to stop doing is being so hard on yourself and doubting yourself. With the two of us working together there's nothing we can't do my love." Her kiss on the cheek was more than reassuring.

Thomas smiled broadly.

"What's so funny?"

"I wasn't laughing at you T I just remember mama telling papa the same exact thing. Thomas pulled the woman beside him hugging her even harder. Laying back with Tanya at his side he

86

felt relieved for the first time in who knows how long. And then almost as if Lucifer had revoked his decree for peace he heard what could only be a revolver followed by another quick burst.

Both were now on their feet. Thomas slid his holster on.

"No," Tanya screamed at Thomas. "You have to learn to delegate Thomas. Let Dante and Dido handle it. Your concern is going to be the death of you."

"You're right," Thomas said sliding his gun back into his holster and putting the gun back behind his head. "But what if it's serious?"

"If it's serious a runner will be here momentarily. C'mon sweetheart. Let Dante do what you appointed him to do. Have a little faith in him. He can handle it."

"I suppose you're right." Thomas said kissing the woman next to him before closing his eyes.

88

Chapter 6

The next morning started as the previous night had ended with a steady staccato of gun fire. Only it was clear that these shots did not emanate from a single revolver but rifle fire that was steady and intense. Before he had a chance to grab his shirt a messenger stood before him. Thomas glanced around him quickly only to find Tanya gone.

"Uncle Thomas, suh, I've been told to tell you that we are under attack by Border Ruffians. Uncle Dido said to tell you that there looks to be no less than a thousand men—excuse me—a battalion and they're on the banks of the river making it impossible to cross.

"Thanks Ned. You did well son," Thomas patted Nat on the shoulder.

"Can I go Uncle Thomas? I'm almost sixteen."

"Not this time, Nat." Thomas said before slapping the boy's horse on the backside and sending him on his way.

So, these so-called Border Ruffians were set on making trouble. Thomas was forced to smile. They obviously didn't know who or what they were up against.

"What's up D?"

"Same ol'. Same ol'. Some Southern fellas just tryin' to show their loyalty to the cause. Little Bear and Dull Knife have taken a battalion across the river a mile or so up river. We're just waitin' for them to launch an all-out offensive before we jump in."

"And the girls?"

"Don't see any need for them. No snipers needed although I do expect a fair amount of casualties in this one. We'll be in close and I can already see some hand-to-hand fighting. Should be a good test for our boys but like I said there should be a fair amount of casualties."

Relieved Tanya was out of danger Thomas took the binoculars from D.

"I see they have two cannons trained on us from across the river."

"Making it certain suicide to even think about crossing the river but they're waiting for us to try and mount a charge. Our job is to keep them distracted just long enough for us to hit 'em hard from behind. A battalion from the front and one from the back and we should wipe them out. Once we hit them from the back they'll swing both the howitzer and the cannons around and we'll hit their flanks and their rear."

"Sounds like a plan to me. I knew I had the right man for the job,"

Now it was totally on him. The slightest miscalculation could only result in many of his friends' lives who had become almost family and somehow become his children

91

A messenger came thundering in.

"Suh, the general asked me to inform you that the men are in position and ready to attack."

"Then tell him to commence to attack. We'll join in as soon as I see that you have their full attention. Now go and God be with you," Thomas said lining up his sights. The rider rode off at a gallop.

"Tighten the wagons and make sure all the livestock are within the circle.

"Men, we'll approach once the 2nd Battalion has them turned and distracted. Once you reach the other side take out the Gatling. That and the river are our only real foes. This pack of rag tag, redneck, Rebels aren't close to being in the same shape we're in. What we have to our advantage is that we are in the best physical shape of any army out there because we train harder and spend our every waking hour preparing for days such as this. They don't have the incentive or motivation that we have. We fight for our freedom. We fight for our very lives. And with God the Father on the side of the righteous we can't be anything but victorious."

A mighty roar went up from the three thousand men gathered for battle.

A large pop followed by another staccato of popping sounds filled the crisp autumn air as Dante peered across the mighty Mississippi. The Border Ruffians caught with their pants down soon forgot their defense of the folks attempting to cross the river and turned to guard their own rear ends. What went from being an offensive maneuver became a defensive one in order to cover their own asses.

"Move men but slowly, quietly and don't commence firing until there are enough men to present a concerted front. Your first objective should be to disable that Gatling. Disable that Gatling and it will certainly change the whole complexion of things. But more importantly I want you men to stay safe so you can return to your families. More importantly know that I love each and every one of you. Now move out men and be quiet as a church mouse," Dante ordered.

The men were well disciplined and well trained and moved with a quiet stealth never seen from a group so large. Staggered in groups of ten wave after wave of men made their way across the river unnoticed.

In all, close to six hundred men made the crossing before they were detected. By then it was too late and with the blistering fire they laid down, the Rebels had all they could do just to hold their position. And with another battalion on their heels it was less than an hour before the entire battalion of Rebel soldiers were forced to make their escape down the banks of the Mississippi.

When it was over there was a great celebration by all involved and the rest of the evening was spent getting the rest of the supply wagons across the river. When it was all said and done they made camp a good ten miles on the western side of the Mississippi.

All-in-all it was quite an eventful day. Most of the inner circle and a few members of Dante's military council gathered around the fire that night. Little Bear and a few of his more trusted braves also joined them.

"Missed seeing you out there Man. I can't remember the last time I've gone into battle without having you right there by my side."

Thomas stared at the ground. He'd always felt it his duty to fight for his people, for himself but they had taken that away with his new duties.

"Please don't go there D. You don't know how hard it is to keep this one away from the sound of gun fire," Tanya grinned. "Let me tell you a little story. I had this mule once. And you know how stubborn mules can be. Well every week on Wednesdays massa would go into town to get his groceries. Most of the time I would go for him. Well this one particular Wednesday I wasn't feeling well and decided not to go 'til the following day but this ol' stubborn ass mule decided he wasn't havin' that and decided that we were going to town despite my decision not to go.

I tried to convince him that massa was fine and didn't need anything that was so important that we had to go right then and there but he wasn't having it. I don't know what it was," Tanya laughed. "Maybe he had another dumb ass waiting for him. I dunno but he drug me halfway to town before I finally made him understand that there was no need to go.

Had a similar experience with that this morning when Dante, Dido, papa and I all did our damnedest to convince Man that he was no longer needed. You don't know how difficult it was to explain everyone's roles to them. General's lead. Soldier's fight. Heads of state run the state but seldom do I see them on the front lines. We all explained this to him but as soon the love of my life heard rifle fire he was up and at 'em."

Everyone had to laugh.

"Man is still a soldier, a warrior at heart. You if anyone should know how hard he worked and trained for that and I for one missed having our finest soldier on the field next to me today." Dante said in defense of his friend. "Just having Man on the field boosts the men's morale. You should know that better than anyone T."

"Oh, c'mon D. Lighten up. In my opinion you didn't need half the troops you had there today. The way you manhandle those

Border Ruffians today. Oh, and by the way, Dido just informed me that we only had one casualty today."

"One's too many," Dante quipped.

"I see you're in a foul mood so I'm just going to leave you alone D. You think you'd be a little more cheerful after such a glorious victory today."

"Perhaps in all of years we've been in the same camp there's one thing you've missed. I don't like killing. And what is worse than taking another's life is having to go to one of my men's wives' or mother's and telling them that he won't be coming home for dinner."

Thomas seeing the tension growing between two of his loved ones was about to intervene when Roman Nose rode in and getting down from his horse said.

"You're right my friend. There's no way you can lessen the loss of life even with such a glorious victory as we shared

98

today. I know how you feel. I've felt the same way on many an occasion and no matter how many times you go through it doesn't get any easier. Still, we must not let it make us bitter and we cannot dwell on it. If we do IT will eat us alive. We must look at it as being God's will. But for now it is time to celebrate a good victory against evil men," Roman Nose said hugging his friend. "C'mon D. Let's drink and smoke. Who knows what tomorrow may bring. But today I toast you my brother. You planned and fought a good fight my friend!"

"Thank you my brother!"

It was then that Nat walked up.

"Mama wants you to come home. She says you need your rest papa," the young man said hugging each of the people before him before helping Dante to his feet.

"I guess the ol' woman knows best," Dante said. "Good night."

There was a quiet pall that descended over the group upon Dante's departure.

"He may be too good a man to lead," Roman Nose commented. "He has a conscience. Not good for a man who has to send other men to their deaths."

"It is never easy to lead," Tanya added.

"But he'll grow into it." Thomas acknowledged.

"We will all grow into it." Roman Nose added.

Chapter 7

The morning came too early to most of the inhabitants of Maroons. The battle had taken its toll on everyone. Crossing the great river had only led to their exhaustion. The new day only led to more unexpected queries on what awaited them in these foreign lands with its unpredictable nature and unforeseen foes.

"Morning son," papa said greeting his son on the way back from the stream on the outskirts of the camp.

"Morning papa."

"Yesterday proved quite an eventful day," the old man said smiling. "How are you holding up Thomas?"

"I'm blessed father."

"Yes, you are. And I pray you never take those blessings for granted. Tell me. How far from our destination are we?"

"Roman Nose says we can start looking for land in the next week or so. Says this is the land that President Lincoln has designated for homesteading but we are still too close to white folks to want to settle this land although it appears to be rich. He seems to think that there are better lands ahead where we will not be bothered at all though. Says the land on the other side of Indian Territory is rich and plentiful."

"And that is where the real work will begin."

"Yes, father but you know we have never been afraid of hard work."

Two weeks later, Tanya and Thomas sat high atop of a ridge overlooking the valley below. A wonderful apple orchard stood at the head of the valley. A small, rambling, brook ran alongside the orchard.

"Oh, Thomas. It's absolutely beautiful. Adam and Eve's Eden couldn't have been any more beautiful. We can build our house there and papa's house over there," she pointing excitedly.

Thomas couldn't help but smile.

"I'll have the carpenters begin tomorrow. I only hope that we can be in before winter sets in."

"Most of the people have already begun building."

"This is good but we must register our deeds if we are to assume legal ownership."

"We'll ride in tomorrow and register and in the meantime I'll have the carpenters start on the house."

"Oh, Thomas,'" Tanya said resting her head on Thomas' massive shoulders. "I'm so happy. For once we can have a place we can really call home, a place we can call our own." It was the happiest Thomas had seen Tanya since mama's passing.

"And you're sure you're ready for Saturday?"

"Now, of that I'm not really sure," she teased.

"What do you mean you're not sure?"

"Well, when we started out I was sure. But since our journey began I haven't seen you. I hardly know you anymore," she joked.

"But baby now that we're settled and have a home together we'll see each other all of the time."

"I hear you but there's no guarantee of that with you being the mayor, president and commander-in-chief," she teased.

Grasping for anything to keep her and not realizing she was pulling his leg he stated matter-of-factly.

"I'll resign. I never asked for this anyway," he replied.

"You could never do that. It's your birthright. Let me see you tell papa you resigned. I'd love to be a fly on the wall when you tell him that one. But seriously and all jokes aside I've been ready and waiting to be your wife since I was sixteen. Of course I'm ready for Saturday, silly."

"But tomorrow we'll register our claims and call for a town meeting to discuss our claims. After that I want to inform the community on how our law proceeds and what will and will not be tolerated in Maroon, as well as the need for quarterly taxes and the enforcement of these laws."

"And how will you enforce these laws?"

"Before I even get to that there's something I've been meaning to speak to about. You see Dante has the army so intent on training, and protecting us against any outside threat and he also is responsible for my security and the security of the inner council so I can't really impose on him anymore. Aside from that most of those working for him have families."

"What are you getting at Thomas?"

"Well, I was considering your girls and since most of them are single..."

"Except for Helen."

"Yeah, except for Helen. But I was thinking that I have a way they could better serve the community and draw a salary as well. What I had in mind was a police force for Maroon."

Tanya smiled.

"Always thinking aren't you?" Tanya smiled.

"Just exploring ways of bettering us as a people and a community is all."

"No need to apologize. That's one of the reasons I accepted your proposal. I like a thinking man but anyway I'll run it by the girls. I think they'll jump at the opportunity. And if you don't mind me asking where do we get the money to pay them?"

"Taxes baby," Thomas grinned.

"And what do we have to tax?"

"My goodness gal! You didn't ask me that! I believe I went through this before but let me refresh your memory. Taxes baby! And I know your next question is what are we taxing? Why you're being taxed for merely being a member of the Maroon community. You're being taxed for your freedom, for your food, your education. Those are just a few of the reasons you're being taxed. Those are just a few of the amenities for being a member of the Maroon community.

If anyone has issues with that they are free to seek residence elsewhere and I'm sure some will test this and venture out to fend for themselves but I think the majority who have come to call Maroon home will have the good sense to accept this without question.

Dido seem to think that those who choose to leave will simply move outside of our jurisdiction and will in turn be our first line of defense. I'm not wishing or hoping for this but it is true.

In any case, the taxes will pay for your girl's service and a host of other things we need including a school, a church and a hospital just to name a few things.

Now come on. We have a long day ahead of us," Thomas helped Tanya to her feet and walked her to her hut before kissing her deeply and passionately.

"And just think after Saturday I won't have to take this long walk," he grinned.

'After Saturday I'll find something else for you to do besides just walk me," she grinned kissing him goodnight.

Chapter 8

Topeka in 1864 was a rough, little, backwoods, cow town at best with cow hands, drifters and homesteaders looking for a brand new start in the uncharted west. It brought hope for the hopeless and a new beginning for those who hadn't fared well east of the Mississippi. For those traveling with the Maroon village it was a new chance at freedom and liberty.

It was a land of Free-State men as well as Pro-Slavers. Still, and all it gave the inhabitants more than a fighting chance to declare a home of their own. Now decked in all black with black face masks that made them that much more sinister and commanding Tanya and Thomas rode into Topeka that blustery cold morning with the sole intent of registering their land deeds as homesteaders.

Quite a formidable front they did present and many of the townspeople seeing an all-Black militia dressed as they were ran for cover. Ignoring the chaos and confusion they'd brought upon the town Thomas calmly dismounted and walked into the sheriff's office.

"Morning suh. I'm trying to find the land office. We're homesteaders hoping to register our claims under The Homestead Act."

The sheriff peeked through the blinds before him and was thrown off guard by the sight before him. Doing his best to regain his composure he did his best to tone down his usual blustery demeanor.

"Listen here boy. I don't know where y'all got yo' information from but homesteadin' don't include no niggas. It states clearly that it's solely for U.S. citizens and from my best recollection niggas ain't considered citizens. Now if y'all still need the land office I can point it out to you."

Before he had a chance to Tanya advanced on the sheriff. Knowing her only too well and expecting trouble Dante pulled down the shades but before he could get the last shade down Tanya administered a swift blow to the sheriff's temple from the butt of her rifle knocking the sheriff down.

"There are no niggas present here suh unless you referring to yourself. The man you are speaking to is known as Thomas Man. When addressing him I'd appreciate it if you would refer to him as Mr. Man. Now if you would please rephrase your statement and I suggest you use my suggestion or I promise I won't be quite as nice next time."

The look she gave the sheriff let him know the woman had little compassion for him, his skin or his office.

"I'm sorrow Mr. Man but the Homestead Act as I know it doesn't apply to Coloreds."

"Much better sheriff but I feel little compassion for redneck Crackers who seem to think they can bully the less fortunate. And I don't believe you were as sincere as you attempted to portray." And with that said Tanya came down once again with the butt of her rifle against the man's temple knocking him unconscious. Dante and Man said nothing.

"Let's ride," Tanya said to her two cohorts.

Thomas had no better luck at the land office but with Tanya's prodding he held his head high on the march back home.

"We have never been given anything," Tanya shouted to the twelve or thirteen thousand at the town meeting the following evening. "We have always had to take everything that truly mattered to us. We had to take our liberty, our freedom. Nothing worth having was ever given to us. Now we must take this land

112

and claim it as ours. They say it is not for Coloreds, that we are not entitled to it so we must claim it and protect it with our lives. Nothing was ever given to us. But our army, the best army this side of the Mississippi will defend and protect this land, our land, from anyone who says otherwise.

Hearing Tanya's declaration to take the land and defend it with their lives the crowd went wild. In essence, it was a call to arms and paved the way for Thomas to institute the laws and taxes with only minor grumblings. Most understood the need and readily accepted the new tariffs with only a handful of families—and not nearly as many as was expected—who chose to leave the quiet confines of Maroon and venture out on their own.

Later, that night and as well the meeting went Dido still seemed upset.

"If five thousand had seen fit to leave it would have at least solidified our perimeter that much more. It would almost have been like having a human moat," he stammered loudly.

Tanya had to laugh.

"Do you even realize that it's people, our folks that you're using as your human moat? These are not pawns in a chess game. These are people, our people, Dido."

"I'm just sayin'. Maroon would have been a lot easier to defend. As it is we'll have difficulty defending ourselves until we have time to shore up our defenses and you know that Cracker sheriff is probably planning and attack right now to drive us out."

"We're working as you speak at strengthening our defenses Dido but I must agree with Tanya on this one. We can't use our people as human sacrifices," Dante said.

A calming voice interrupted the discussion.

"Today in Topeka I met a man. He was a white man like so many others I've met. And from what I could gather this white man believes like so many of them believe that their birthright alone makes them better than any Niggra. He didn't exactly say that being that he witnessed the 1st Battalion in full battle regalia and in all their glory and then was faced with T who was not in one of her better moods.

But now that he has time to sit back and think. Now that he has time to sit back and reflect I'm sure that he will go about trying to organize a force of equal strength and I'm also sure if my intuition is correct that we will be receiving a visit from him and his like-minded cohorts in the weeks to follow. They will be here for one purpose and one purpose only and that will be to put us back in what they see are our rightful places and that place ain't out here on his plains claimin' to be homesteadin'. Like I said we should be receiving a visit from him within the upcoming weeks.

"Well, with the mountains at our backs and the river protecting us we can use the same tactics we used when we were in the swamps. We can use the natural terrain as a large part of our defense."

"Or we can invite them in and ambush the hell out of them." Dante added taking Thomas prognosis to the next level.

"I like that. Especially the part about letting them in and ambushing the hell out of them," she grinned. Her girls hadn't seen action in months and were chomping at the bit in anticipation. "We can set up my sharpshooters and snipers in tree stands along the road preventing any escape and keeping them in the snare."

"Sorry T but I'm not sure we can have you involved in anymore skirmishes or out-in-out battles.

"What the hell are you talking about D?"

"Let's just say we were in the old country T. Thomas would be the equivalent of a king making you his queen. The king

116

and queen are never on the front lines. After all, when all is said and done neither can be exposed to warfare but must be made to remain in a safe haven where they can rule when the fighting is over."

Tanya couldn't help but laugh.

That may be correct D. but this is not the old country and if I recollect correctly papa and mama were king and queen and papa led the army and mama started the women's unit."

"I mean no disrespect T but where is mama now? My point exactly and as much as it hurts me the people of Maroon need your guidance more than your gun at this point."

Looking at Thomas for support and seeing that he would not come to her defense she sat down dejectedly.

"Let me be clear so all here understand this latest proclamation. Following your wedding on Saturday you will appoint someone to replace you as captain of the women's contingent. You will however continue in your new role as sheriff and police chief."

Tanya nodded but was noticeably shaken by the earlier decree. And after the countless hours she'd spent training her girls she'd been relegated to advisor if that. It was all a bit much but then wasn't she who'd crowed about how she'd had to almost hog chain Thomas to be still when he'd been relieved of his command.

In the meantime, Dante and Thomas spent the remainder of the week shoring up the perimeter defenses and setting up booby-traps over the vast expanse of exposed perimeter. They then placed soldiers at integral intervals making sure every avenue was covered.

Tanya spent her time helping Helen, the new commander of the women's unit staging her band of women sharpshooters and snipers where they would have a clear but covered line of fire.

It was now Wednesday, three days after their venture into Topeka.

"See if you can't get a couple of souls to go into Topeka and see what's going on. The more time they have the larger their forces will be if I'm guessing right." Dante said to Helen after dinner.

"I'll get on it first thing in the morning sweetie," she replied after the kids were in bed. "You know I was just thinking D and I don't want you to get all bent out of shape by what I'm about to say but do you realize that when T abdicates her role on Saturday and I take over the women's unit that you and I will be in control of the total army of Maroon and I'm in no way suggesting anything but the United States Army is the only army larger on this continent. If we had a mind to, we could run over half of these little one horse, Cracker towns and be rich beyond our means."

"We certainly could but I suspect we have enough trouble here just trying to ward off that kind of thing. Besides I'm quite happy just trying to take over Helen and this army of kids I have. And having them already makes me rich beyond my wildest dreams."

"You're a good man D. I guess I was just dreaming wide awake. The good Lord has certainly blessed me with you sweetie. You keep me grounded when I get to daydreaming and fantasizing and I love you for that."

"I've had the same thoughts but never would I want that. In fact I'm not sure I want the role I've been given. You know with much power comes much responsibility. You're about to find that out sweetheart."

And with that said he found his rifle, his pipe and headed for the council fire.

"You sit alone my friend. You seem to have a lot on your mind."

"I suppose I do."

"We're fine Man. We can hold our own against any local militia."

"I'm not worried about us holding our own or defending ourselves against anyone. With you at the helm that's the least of my worries."

"I'm glad you have such confidence in me but then what is it that has my brother sitting out here all alone on a night such as this? Could it be we are having second thoughts about tying the knot," Dante teased.

Thomas stirred the dying embers of the fire with a stick. Pulling out a nice wad of tobacco Dante tore off a plug before handing it to Thomas who tore off a healthy piece of his own and inserted it into his mouth. Chewing it for a while poking the fire at regular intervals it was obvious he had a lot on his mind and was trying his best to sort it out. It was some time before he spoke.

"You know I took your advice and handed it up to God. And then I prayed. And I can honestly say the last three months have been pure heaven to me. I made the call and didn't engage the women on the trail here."

"With Roman Noses' braves as escorts there were no engagements, no skirmishes. Even without their help who would attack a party as large as ours? They'd have to be damn fools. Anyway, it's been made clear that following your wedding T is to relinquish all of her military directives. She knows that and seems fine being our first constable. She seems fine and will do well defining the position."

"All of that's true D and I have little or no qualms with that. It's not that but let me ask you a question. Do you know Helen? I mean do you really know your woman?"

"Probably not half as well as you know T since I didn't grow up in the same house as Helen," D smiled.

"That's the thing. Yeah, we grew up in the same house but with two different teachers. Mama raised T and we all know how she came to meet her maker."

"You do know what they say Thomas."

"No. What's that?"

"A man who has nothing to die for has nothing to live for," Dante concluded.

"I gotcha but what I'm havin' a hard time understanding is something others have noticed and addressed as well. Just the other day Monique and a few of the other girls were just sitting around talking when they just happened to bring up the skirmish with the Colonel and their final day when three or four of them including the Colonel were sentenced to hang. Seems they were all executed but not as sentenced. You see they weren't hung. Instead their throats were cut."

"And? I don't get it. What's the problem? An execution is an execution. They're not fun for anyone."

"I understand that. D. The problem is that the executioner was Tanya. She's the person who slit their throats."

"It's obvious that she has some deep-seated hatred for white folks. I only wish she were still fighting alongside me. She's a born leader and would help alleviate a lot of responsibility."

"You're not getting my point D. They say she executed twelve other men in the same manner when we fought the Colonel."

"My response to you is to dwell on the positive, on what you can control. The bottom line and the truth of the matter is that she loves you more than anyone I've seen. She would go to the ends of the earth for you. Now if you ever were to cross her well," he said grinning broadly, "that's another story.

What she does in times of battle can be excused but you or I may never know or be able to explain where her hatred emanates from. Here's a woman that was raised by your parents because both of her parents were victims of this peculiar institution. And you wonder why she has such hatred for white folks. Can you tell me why these Crackers have such a deep-seated hatred for Niggras? You probably can't. What's worse is that they can't say either. Hers is simply a response to their hatred.

Listen, we can't always see a reason for the things we do. In that case, what I suggest you do is accept that that we cannot change and give it up to God and remember the bottom line is that her love for you is unwavering. That's a fact you cannot question my brother."

"I suppose you're right again my friend. Thanks for always putting things in proper perspective."

"Not a problem but I'd still sleep with one eye open," Dante laughed. "But trust me you will soon see things a lot clearer. You see even a good marriage will age you and with age comes wisdom. When you question a woman's motives for doing something first ask how her actions will affect you. If they don't affect you and she's acting out of her own passion then ignore it. Just let it go."

"It's funny though D. We talk about everything. But she's never talked about any of this and when I bring it up she blows it off and shows little or no remorse."

"Let it go Man."

"But…"

"Let it go," Dante pulled out a flask and passed it to Thomas.

An hour later neither man felt any pain when a rider rode up.

"Suh. There's a group of riders at the front gate and the man in charge is somewhat adamant about speaking to 'The Head Nigga in Charge" of this 'rag tag outfit', the young man grinned.

"That would be you," Dante said turning to Thomas. "But being this late at night I can assume it is not to share pleasantries over tea so I will handle it. But what you can do is alert the second and third battalions to get into position. Now go home and get some rest. From what I understand you have a big day ahead of you tomorrow."

Turning to the young man at his right Dante sent forth the directive.

"William send out word that the 1st and 4th battalions should assemble in full gear on the courtyard at the gate."

"Yes sir, general."

No sooner than the young man was out of sight than a shadow appeared from the very same darkness.

"I tried to get some sleep but with all the commotion and riders riding up to the house it was next to impossible. What's going on?" Tanya struggled to wipe the sleep from her eyes.

"Not exactly sure yet. A rider just came in. That's probably who awoke you."

"A rider at this time of night? It can only be trouble."

"You must have been eavesdropping. That's just what I told your other half before I sent him on his way."

"Seriously though, what's up D?"

"Riders. Don't know how many but there seeking 'the head nigga in charge'."

"Oh. Lawd! More Crackers! Why can't they just leave us alone? Is there a place on earth where Colored folks can live in peace?" Tanya screamed.

"C'mon T. I don't know that there is but what I do know is that anything worth having is worth fighting for. And this land is ours and we ain't gonna let no overzealous mob take it from us." Dante proclaimed mounting his horse and heading for the front gate.

"I'm riding with you," Tanya shouted racing for her horse.

"But I thought we had an agreement," Thomas shouted at his wife to be.

"Our agreement begins on Saturday," she smiled before leaning down from her saddle and kissing him on the cheek then heading in the same direction Dante had ridden. As she rode men in black uniforms joined her riding in from the countryside.

By the time Tanya reached the front gate well over two thousand men had gathered waiting to receive their orders. At the same time her women awaited her arrival.

A white man under a white flag rode into a sea of darkness.

"Who's in charge here?" The rather staunch man with the receding hairline and red beard asked as he rode in.

"I believe you're looking for 'the head nigga in charge'. That is the message we received from your messenger. Would you care to rephrase your request sir?"

The man looked out and as far as he could see were dark faces in dark uniforms riding in. Still, the man's pride would not allow him to lose face in front of these niggras.

"Whatever. Is you the one in charge here boy?"

"No suh. The man in charge is attending to more pressing business and does not have time for a bunch of red-necked

130

Crackers at this late hour. However, my cohorts here can answer any questions you may have. You see I am here to represent the good people of Maroon. Now what is it I can do for you sheriff? And be careful of how you address us and the tone in which you speak. I would hate to have to make your wife a widow." Dante said smiling.

"I know you niggas think you can…" Dante backhanded the sheriff with hardly any effort but blow sent the man reeling a good six or seven feet from where he'd been standing. The sheriff stunned beyond belief stared up at the six foot four Black man glowering down at him.

"All I ask is the same thing my friend asked you in your office in Topeka. How quickly you forget or are you just slow and feebleminded? If that is the case then I will ask you once again that you treat me with the same respect that I show you when I speak to you. You may want to keep your personal feelings in tow when here. Don't and you may meet a fate far harsher than what has just occurred. Now you were saying?"

"The land you niggras is on is government land and under the law you niggras don't qualify to homestead. Therefore and as a representative of the federal government in these here parts I'm going to need you and yours to vacate this land within the week."

"Excuse me suh but we are a day's ride from Topeka. Are you even in your jurisdiction or is this some personal crusade to keep Niggras out in your pursuit to help make Kansas a slave state?"

Rising to his feet and securing his holster he dusted his trousers off and turned to face the taller man.

"Damn you niggas. The people of Topeka want the likes of y'all gone and as a representative of this territory I must ask for y'all to be gone by the end of the week," The scarlet faced sheriff shouted to all listening. "Is that understood?"

132

Dante smiled at the agitated man.

"Or?" Dante said raising his hands and signaling the three thousand soldiers to come out of the shadows and into plain view. The sheriff now saw a force that tripled the one that had made its presence known in Topeka two weeks earlier. The sheriff was stunned by the numbers of Black soldiers dressed in their all black regalia.

"Sheriff suh, my people have traveled a long ways to reach this land that promised a new beginning. All we ask is to be left alone to live in peace," Dante said to the stunned man.

"Look nigga I'm bein' nice in givin' y'all a week. One week nigga! One week!"

"Well, in that case, and if you can't see fit to change your mind suh, then there is no need to wait a week. I can tell you that my folks are tired of running. This is our land and we will defend it with our lives if need be."

It was at this juncture that Tanya rode in.

"We've got them boxed in. There's no escape. Just say the word and let the games begin." Tanya said her eyes fixated on Dante. At the same time a rather large contingent of black hooded men encircled the sheriff.

"What you mean is let the killing begin," Dante said shifting his gaze from the sheriff to the newly appointed queen who sat upon her horse in such a regal manner that everyone in attendance was enamored by her mere presence.

"Just say the word D. and we'll annihilate these Crackers," Tanya said. There was no play in her voice. She was, if nothing else, an elite soldier besting most of the soldiers she fought alongside of. But her most acknowledged attribute was her exotic good looks which made most of the men folk in the village take a second look even though they were familiar with seeing her on a daily basis. Her well chiseled Roman nose stood thin and pointy unlike most of the inhabitants of the colony whose flatter, broader noses spoke of their true African heritage. Her full red lips let everyone know that that her African heritage was in at least partial evidence from whose roots she'd evolved. But it was her chocolate mocha complexion that led everyone she came into contact with know that her genes had been tampered with in some way. And anyone who'd ever came into contact with the Spanish swore that she was Spanish or of Spanish descent. What she was in essence was one of the most beautiful women in Maroon but what really separated her from other women was the way in which she carried herself. Mama used to always say that she was of royal descent.

Standing at a shade under six feet she was stately, almost noble in bearing. Yet, despite her majestic attributes she remained humble garnering the respect of the community.

But now she stood before her general who openly admonished her for suggesting the massacre of these men.

"There will be no killing today. The sheriff will take his men back to Topeka and I will give him one week to rethink his decision on putting us off our lands but there will be no killing and carnage tonight. Is that understood?"

Tanya dropped her head in acknowledgement before addressing the sheriff who remained mute in awaiting his verdict.

"Stay off our land you racist, in-bred, bastard," she said riding up to the sheriff and knocking him to the ground before turning her horse and galloping off in the direction of home.

"I don't believe she's too fond of you," Dante said laughing as the sheriff scrambled to get to his feet.

The rest of the week was a myriad of hustle and bustle throughout the community with most of the inhabitants working on preparation for the upcoming wedding. At any time of day a bevy of carpenters often numbering thirty or more and other skilled laborers worked night and day building the palatial home for the newlyweds. When it was finished many said the magnificent structure could rival any of the great Southern estates. The home complete with indoor plumbing, running water, a colossal wine cellar and balconies and fireplaces in almost all the bedrooms. The library came complete with everything from cookbooks to de Tocqueville's democracy in America. A separate bedroom for papa closely resembled the master bedroom with its own balcony and fireplace and was there should papa get lonely and want to spend some time or just come visit from time-to-time.

It seemed everyone was cooking or baking something and the wedding seemed to work as not only a partnership between a man and a woman but the inauguration and coronation of the colony. For everyone it was a new beginning.

On Saturday everyone who could attend did so. In all, it was a glorious occasion with good food, ample spirits and a renewed sense of hope.

Dante and Thomas now hoped that as winter grew closer and the people were now comfortably tucked in their fine homes that they'd be able to concentrate on other more pressing community issues such as building a school, a church and finding a way to provide for the less fortunate.

"I think perhaps it's time for a town hall meeting," Thomas mused as he sat on his front porch one evening with his most trusted confidante Dante.

"For what? Folks are good. They're warm, their bellies are full, and they have no fear. What is there to discuss? I think you should leave well enough alone my brother." Dante replied as Thomas chuckled.

"You are becoming more and more cynical my friend. I just want to meet with them to reassure them that we are here for them should they have any pressing needs or concerns during the winter."

"I think that's a splendid idea my husband. I think you should also tell the people to stay on full alert at all times and to inform those in authority that if they encounter anything out of the ordinary to report it immediately. It has been quiet for far too long."

"Very true and you know there will be repercussions and retaliation from that Cracker after you kicked and knocked the pride and arrogance out of his Southern ass," Dante said laughing and spilling the tobacco from his pipe.

"Duly noted," he said winking at his bride. "We'll call for a town meeting tomorrow. But for now I must wish you all a good night. I'm bushed. Oh, and D can you check in on papa on your way in?"

"Not a problem Man. Night."

On cue Tanya got up wished everyone a good night and followed Thomas to the house.

"Talk about a marriage made in heaven," Dido said poking the fire. "And nothing's changed as far as I can see."

"Trust me. Things have changed," Dante smiled and glanced at Helen who suddenly rose to her feet.

"And I think it may be high time we headed home as well," she said grabbing her husband's and pulling him to his feet.

Meanwhile, in the master bedroom, Thomas threw more kindling on the dying fire.

"Please sweetheart. I'm tired enough already," she said staring at the broad shouldered, barrel chested man in front of her.

T could feel the heat emanating from her loins and when she could no longer look at the muscular stature before she let her petticoat fall to the floor and said.

"Take me my husband.

Chapter 9

Up at the break of dawn the next morning Thomas was emblazoned with hope for not only himself but more importantly his people, his community. They'd fought off many a formidable adversary and escaped virtually unscathed in search for their own. And after months of traveling, they'd found a land that instilled a certain hope in them. If nothing else, they were free with an infinite amount of possibilities.

On his way downstairs that morning he smiled broadly and stopped to give pause as well as to thank His most high for the blessing that had been bestowed on him. Tanya had always been there and their union brought about a treasure trove of pleasures he could never have imagined. Well, that is when she wasn't totally exhausted from acting as sheriff and teacher.

It was now going on two wheels since the sheriff had issued his decree and though everyone went on with life as usual the sheriff's decree remained in the back of everyone's mind.

"I guess that sheriff had enough sense to call off his dogs." Tanya noted after dinner.

"I think D's show of strength that day was all the deterrent needed but don't count him out quite yet. Dante showing them our forces may have had a dual effect. It was definitely a deterrent that day but it also gives them concern. Now they know they must bring a force large enough to subdue us. Folks out here are farmers for the most so it will take him some time to amass a force to contest one of our strength. But like I said, don't count him out. Hatred is a powerful motivator."

"On that I would have to agree." Tanya said grabbing her shawl. "Time for the town meeting," she said kissing him on his cheek.

144

Overall, the meeting went well with the only disagreement arising over the matter of the Topeka threat.

"I think we need to send someone in there to live and work for two or three months at a time to keep tabs on the situation," an older member suggested.

"No, no, no. I say we stay away from Topeka. They know how we look and haven't been back since. They're not coming back. They're full of hate but they didn't strike me as being suicidal." Papa's friend ol' Sam commented.

"I will keep your suggestions in my mind and I agree that putting someone in Topeka would be wise as well as Lawrence. With the threat of war on the horizon, I think it is important we stay abreast of the unions efforts. After all their efforts are on our behalf.

Right now colored soldiers aren't being allowed to fight but once President Lincoln signs the orders and colored soldiers are allowed to fight we need to know and be ready."

The folks gathered applauded the progress and marveled at the sheer magnificence of the house. That night there was a celebration bestowed on the Indian chief. When it was over Roman Nose had two –not one but two— wagon fills of gifts. And the people thanked him each in their own way for acting as their protector for the three or four months they were on the trail.

Thomas had spent his days on the trail thinking of a night just like this where he would get his chance to properly celebrate his lifelong friend.

"I would just like to thank Roman Nose for always being there and for being my friend. I don't know if y'all realize what was just transpired. This man risked not only his life but the lives of his brave men who like us are also sons, brothers, and fathers.

To assure our safety. I consider you my brother and the Cherokee my family. As long as I have a home you have a home by brother."

The two men embraced for a while and some say that they saw the mighty war chief shed a tear but this has yet to be confirmed. In all it was a wonderful celebration and there were even some who not having anything of value to bestow on the might chief sought other means of pacifying and acknowledging the great chief.

Chasity Pettiway, the comely, mid-thirtyish said something to grab the usually elusive Roman Nose's attention. A former New Orleans entertainer. Folks say she was a very talented singer and dancer who had made a small fortune before opening a very popular establishment on Beale St. Still, she'd never recovered from the fact that her childhood sweetheart remained a slave. This disheartened her greatly so she started saving her money with the hopes of buying her man's freedom and heading out west to start a

147

new life. When his owner refused to sell him at any price the woman was devastated.

But so committed were they to the idea of starting a new life together that they decided to run. When slavers gave chase and began to get close the young man sent his woman one way and drew the slavers to him. And after twice attempting escape he was promptly captured just moments before meeting her and was summarily hung. She'd already liquidated her assets with the idea of them both fleeing and joining Maroon.

In the wake of his death Chastity Pettiway remained strong and steadfast. Never again would she be the victim to love's wrath. After all, she was a Colored woman who by law did not have the right to happiness.

That was three years ago. Since she'd arrived she was seen as being an ideal citizen lending a helping hand with whatever she could help in the community.

Sexy and voluptuous, she kept the men of Maroon heads turning. Yet in the three years she'd been there no one could ever remember seeing her in any man's company.

After a while it was just assumed that the men of Maroon just weren't in the same league as the high falutin' Chastity Pettiway. But it was she who approached the highly celebrated war chief of the Southern Cheyenne.

That night several hundred of Roman Nose's braves lay just on the outskirts of the colony awaiting their chief. And thank God they did. From all accounts gunshots could be heard throughout the entire vastness that was Maroon. It was Roman Nose's braves that saved the day. Unorthodox in their fighting strategy and comfortable enough in guerilla warfare they harassed the cavalry intent on catching Maroon with their pants down. By the time the cavalry recovered Maroon's lines were solidly in place.

In the thirty years in existence it was the first time Maroon had taken on a contingent as large as their own. The Maroon army held its own for most of the day. With the evening, however, one could feel the tide beginning to turn.

With a thousand braves engaged in the affair Roman Nose sent wave after wave to strike at the soldier's flanks and rear which was used more or less to diminish the morale and confuse them. But these were like no troops Thomas or Dante had ever encountered before. These federal troops were both disciplined and well-trained staying in formation and never really coming undone despite the Indians furious attacks.

Tanya's sniper unit now led by Helen were unable to get a clear shot as the U.S. troops who did not panic or run for cover. Dug in quite well they could neither advance nor really gain a decisive edge. In all, both Maroon battalions and the cavalry both fought valiantly and sustained minimal casualties although on this night Maroon suffered more casualties than they'd suffered in all previous battles combined.

A sustained and aggressive attack from the rear may have overcome the cavalry's relentless bombardment but the Indians being guerilla fighters did not fight in that manner making it hard to overcome the army they now faced.

Dante had both the 3rd and 4th battalions waiting in the rear and waiting to go but was reluctant to send them in. Seeking his friend's advice Dante found Thomas with the 3rd. Pulling him aside D turned to his friend.

"Should I send them in?"

"Why are you asking me D? This is your army and this is your call."

"I'm asking you because even though we outnumber them we're taking a beating and the casualties are mounting."

"Then by all means send them in. Send in the 3rd. Give it some time. If you don't see a change then send in the 4th as well. We should be coming for a ceasefire for the night. Start positioning them at nightfall so they'll be rested and ready to attack at dawn."

Dante couldn't help but be appreciative. No longer did he have to accept the responsibility of sending these men, his men, to an early grave. As advised D. sent the 3rd and 4th battalions in. He then set a runner to Helen to intersperse her sharpshooters with the 3rd battalion.

It was quiet now. A half an hour later three men appeared on the open field under a white flag or truce.

Dante called for his horse and he and Dino rode across the open prairie to meet them.

"I'm Colonel Chivington and am here under jurisdiction of the federal government. Our reports are that a large number of

Coloreds are homesteading illegally on land set aside for homesteading. We have been told that when local authorities asked you to vacate the premises they were attacked which is why we are here.

"Far too many men have died today. Why don't we end this now? I will give your people one week to leave or we will commence all this needless bloodshed. What do you say suh?"

A few miles away Thomas arrived at his father's cottage.

"How's it going my son?" his father asked.

"I'm not sure papa. The men are fighting well enough but never have they fought anyone of this caliber. The 1st and 2nd suffered heavy casualties. Dante is employing the 3rd and 4th while it's quiet. They'll lead the attack at dawn."

His father lit his pipe and gazed at the fire in the fireplace. It was obvious that his thoughts were deep somewhere else.

"I am sure that by now you understand that we are in a different place than we have ever been. We have always had to fight. Our freedom and independence depended on us defending ourselves against slave owners, slave catchers and local militias. And it's funny but as we grew so did our forces. In reality, there really was no one who actually posed a real or significant threat.

But today we are up against the United States government and even should you win this battle how will you combat them moving forward. If you massacre these men today what will be the repercussions. If the war doesn't happen soon they will be intent on our genocide," Papa said pulling on his pipe slowly, his eyes never leaving the fire.

"It almost appears to be a lose-lose situation," Thomas mused.

"You're damned if you do and damned if you don't."

"If we beat a contingent of the U.S. Army it will read as a massacre of federal troops out on a routine patrol by a bunch of runaway slaves and outlaws on land protected for homesteaders. If we don't defend ourselves we will be sent back to our captors or murdered."

"That's the way it appears."

"What would you suggest Papa?"

"If the war starts tomorrow these same men you fight today would be your allies tomorrow but I cannot predict when the war will begin. They tell me that South Carolina was already seceded. But honestly I see no alternative other than what you're doing. However, I would send Dido to Washington to have him lobby our position. And I'd send him immediately."

"Thank you Papa," Thomas said bending over and hugging the old man. "I love you papa," Thomas added before making his leave and heading back to the front to join Dante.

"Says he'll give us a week to vacate. Told him I had to talk to my people and I'd get back him in an hour."

"Smart. We're going to take that week," Thomas said passing Dante a wad of tobacco to chew on.

"What are you saying, Thomas? Are you saying we're going uproot these poor souls again?"

"Hardly. This is our home and we will fight to keep it. No. We are not going anywhere. We are simply biding our time. The war is going to begin. These same federal troops we fight today will be fightin' on behalf of the Niggra and chances are will be called off to fight.

Here's another potential scenario. Lincoln's on the verge of freeing the slaves and giving us our rights as citizens making us entitled to be homesteaders legally.

In the meantime, I'm sending Dido to Washington to make them aware of what's going on and lobby our cause. Hopefully

156

these men will be pulled away before the week is up," Thomas said spitting into the fire.

"What I've admired about…" Dante smiled.

"What's that, my friend?"

"You can see sunshine in a rain cloud," Dante said continuing to smile.

"Tell the colonel we agree to a week. And bring in as many supplies and munitions as you can and prepare for a prolonged fight."

"Not a problem."

"If you need me I'll be at the house."

Chapter 10

Thomas rode home feeling pretty good despite all the death and killing. The week would give the wounded and infirmed time to heal and regain their battle readiness. Hopefully, this would be the end of this confrontation.

Thomas entered his palatial home.

"Hey sweetheart," Thomas smiled as Tanya grabbed him by the neck and pulled him to her before slapping a passionate kiss upon his lips.

"What was that for?" Thomas asked a puzzled look on his face.

"What? I can't kiss my husband?"

"Never said that. Just wanted to know what I need to do to get more of those more often."

"Oh hush silly. Now tell me. How are we doing?"

"Well, the 1st and 2nd took heavy casualties," Thomas said before updating his wife on everything that had transpired.

"From everything you've told me it seems like this Colonel Chivington seems to be a pretty honorable sort of guy."

"He does. Doesn't seem like he's so much interested in us as colored folk per say as it does with him carrying out his orders."

"Well, you have a week to strategize and get to know your enemy," Tanya mused as she put the ham, collards, candied yams and corn before Thomas. It was then that Thomas had a thought that would change the way in which he the world he'd come to know but that it would have to wait. For now all he saw was his queen standing before him radiant in her glow. There was something different about her tonight though.

"Dinner was delicious T. Is there any way you can duplicate that for guests tomorrow or the day after?"

160

"I suppose I can. Anyone special?"

"I'm thinking the good colonel."

"And what makes you think he'll sit down with Niggras?"

"Don't know that he will. What I do know is that nothing fails but a try and communication is the key to saving lives. He seems to be a man of God as well as a man of peace and cares about the welfare of his men. He'll sit down."

Chapter 11

The following morning, Thomas sent an envoy to the colonel who agreed to meet with the leaders of Maroon the following evening. The rest of the day saw wagon after wagon enter Maroon with supplies and munitions to last the remainder of the winter. It was early February and snow still capped the mountains surrounding Maroon.

A hospital had been in the works along with the school and for the first time it dawned on Thomas as he made his rounds that the hospital was already at its capacity after yesterday's battle and would have to enlarged.

By the end of the day all had been informed of the colonel's demand. Yet, morale remained high with most of the people seeming impervious to the threat the soldiers posed."

"They're so used to us protecting them and them not being threatened that they can't even conceive of a legitimate threat," Tanya commented.

"And I'm going to do everything I can to keep them thinking that way. We'll have a ceremony to honor those who gave their lives, one funeral and a mass burial. We will acknowledge the dead as heroes and martyrs who gave their lives to keep us free. I'd like the colonel to be there followed by dinner."

"I will do my part my husband. Anything else?"

"Yes, I want your girls out-front in full uniform. We're going to put on a little show for the colonel. I would like for him to see some of the finest shooting in the world done by women who they also consider second-class citizens. If nothing else I want this to be an eye opener, a chance for him to see Niggras independent of any government who are prospering peacefully and pushing the envelope."

164

Chapter 12

Thomas and the rest of Maroon slept peacefully that night but with the morning came a burst of enthusiasm as the community went to work or to school.

Many men went hunting as game was plentiful in the nearby forests and steppes. Still others plowed fields in preparation for the spring planting. Women unpacked the last of the winter's canned goods and prepared them for dinner to be accompanied by whatever fresh kill their man brought in from the day's hunt.

Meanwhile, Thomas fed his growing herd of appaloosas. He loved working and breeding his fine line of horses and had all the intentions on selling them once he deemed the herd large enough.

Tanya taught one of the normal elementary school classes and was completely immersed in her children (as she referred to them). When she was finished she would stop by the tiny sheriff's office to make sure things were peaceful among the inhabitants.

Finding everything in order. She led her horse home only to find her girl's already assembling on the front porch. Seeing her each woman to a person hugged her as if she were the prodigal daughter.

"What's up baby girl? We don't see you anymore since you tied the you know what," Diola said.

"I never thought Thomas to be the type to keep his woman tied up."

"Me either and if you don't say anything, I won't either," Tanya whispered. Her girls fell out.

"So you enjoy being married, girl?"

"Now what do you think? I've had a crush on the boy since I was seven. Of course, I love it. Now come on. You're commanding officer is in need of your services."

"What's this all about T?"

"Thomas should be here momentarily. He'll fill you in. In the meantime, you can change in the bedroom. When you're finished changing, there should be food and libations set up for you in the parlor but please don't drink too much. Your services may be on call tonight," Tanya said before going to check on Papa in the library.

An hour later, the colonel rode up in a carriage fit for a king. Stepping down from the carriage the colonel reached for Thomas' hand.

"Colonel Edward Chivington"

"Thomas. Thomas Man. It is indeed a pleasure to make your acquaintance Colonel. I read about your military engagements with plains Indians. Some of your strategies are considered military genius."

"In some eyes, I don't think the Plains Indians would agree," the colonel said somewhat surprised with the Colored man's knowledge.

"I must say, you people have done a magnificent job in creating this community. The houses I saw on the road here would rival any I've seen. And yours is certainly in that category."

"Come let me show you the inside," Thomas said beaming with pride.

The colonel, a rather handsome man in his mid-thirties stepped into the parlor full of T's girls who were suddenly enamored by the colonel.

"Such a handsome devil. I'd hate to have to shoot him."

"You know when it goes down he'll be our primary target."

"No one ever said war was fair," Diola whispered.

Chapter 13

The girls were put in their positions in the front yard where targets were staggered every hundred yards. A squad of five girls were lined up at each target and the command was given.

"Ready, aim, fire!" and the air exploded with puffs of smokes. When the target was reeled in it showed all five shots in the bull's-eye. It was the same at the two hundred and three hundred yards. So impressed by such fine shooting was the colonel that he made it a point to shake each woman's hand thanking them for their performance.

Later that evening, after a splendid dinner and dessert that included three different cakes and a variety of pastries Papa along with Dante, Thomas, Helen and Tanya sat in the parlor with the good colonel.

"So, where ya from colonel." Papa said lighting his cigar.

"Boston suh. Boston, Massachusetts."

"You're a long way from home ain'tcha son?"

"Yes suh and I miss it terribly but I had this hankerin' to see this big beautiful country and service my country so I signed up after college and it led me here."

"Do you have any regrets about your decision?"

"You probably know better than I do papa. Anytime you're in a position of leadership you're faced with tough decisions. And those tough decisions may cause harm and death to others. But then why am I telling you suh. You have been in this position far longer than I."

"The only difference is that my orders come from God above. I will not and have never taken orders from another man to inflict harm or death on any man," papa countered.

"I hear and understand you. This is a most trying time for all of us."

"Yes, they are." Man interjected "But humor me for a minute colonel. Let's say the war breaks out tomorrow. Let's just say. Which side will you fight for?" Thomas queried.

"Why my allegiance will always remain with the North and the Union," the colonel said never giving it a second thought as he sipped his brandy.

'Then if I am hearing you right you're for the liberty and freedom of the Niggra?"

"Yes, I suppose I am."

"Then once the war begins you will fight on our behalf."

"Ad why may I ask will you fight on our behalf and today you attempt to kill us. You see how we live. Why do you seek to stop us from our plight to be free and autonomous? We inflict no

173

harm on threat to anyone. We are isolated, with Topeka being the closest town and we are self-sufficient. If I lied or embellished in any way please stop me."

"No, Man I think you have been accurate in your dedication and my heart goes out to you and yours. I see what you have created here and it is both marvelous and magnificent. The abolitionist from home would have a field day with Maroon as an example of what the Niggra can achieve."

"And having said all that are you still insisting that we leave in a week?" Thomas asked knowing now that the good colonel, a northerner from the liberal state of Massachusetts couldn't possibly follow through with more carnage and death after having come to know his enemy.

Thomas smiled as he awaited the colonel's reply. It had always been a gift, the fast that he could usually get a fairly accurate read on most people. And if he'd ascertained anything in the past four or five hours it was that Colonel Chivington was a fair and reasonable man.

"As much as it bothers me to say this I must follow orders. I will send correspondence back to Washington giving an account on what I witnessed here. But we may not hear back for weeks. In the meantime, I must follow my orders."

"But…" Thomas started.

"Stop," Papa interjected, "The man is a soldier. It is obvious the colonel has a conscience. His hardest fight will not be with our demise but living with the fact the he was responsible for it. But enough talk of war and dying. Let us both friend and foe celebrate this day of peace and Gods' presence.

"Salud," said the colonel holding up his glass of brandy.

Chapter 14

Man and the colonel met several more times over the next week to speak on a variety of subjects ranging from DaVinci's genius to the Rebs chances in the impending war.

What was obvious is that the two men had a genuine like and respect for each other. Papa noted that in a different world things may have been different. In a different world the two men may have been the best of friends.

"So, let me see if I understand. A group of white citizens led by Topeka's sheriff rides into the fort and states that there is a large group or Coloreds in uniform and bearing army that are squatting on government land despite orders to leave and you come out here to force us to either leave or annihilate us."

The good colonel paused before speaking.

"That's not exactly what happened. You see the sheriff has friends in high places in Washington it seems. We received word that a large Colored army was squatting on government lands right outside and were threating to raid the town Topeka. No mention was made of the hundred or so miles distance from Topeka.

But the real reason we were sent is that your organization and sheer numbers pose a threat to whites."

That was on Sunday evening April 10th the last day of the week long cease fire. On Monday morning Colonel Chivington sent an envoy to Thomas inquiring as to their time of departure.

"Sir, I must inform you that despite our previous conversations the people have chosen to stay saying that this land belongs to them and they will defend it with their lives."

The envoy returned with no other correspondence.

At 9a.m. the first cannon fire was heard followed by a crescendo of small arm's fire. The colonel believing he had been duped into believing that this could have a peaceful ending threw everything he had at the Colored army in the first few hours. In the days prior to the attack Dante had repositioned his army so they were out of range of the colonel's artillery. When the colonel's men tried to close the gap Helen and her team of snipers would pick them off one at a time. During this furious barrage by the cavalry it was obvious that the tide had turned once again. And when the third battalion hit them from the rear everyone knew that it was a done deal. The battle was for all intents and purposes over.

Dante sent a runner to Man with the message.

"We are victorious against our toughest foe thus far, The United States Army. There are perhaps two hundred who remain captive, including the colony who has a mild injury. What would you have me do with them?"

Thomas handed Tanya the note. It was clear, she was visibly shaken. She then handed the note to Papa whose expression remained the same. "Tanya," Thomas said staring at his wife.

"No mercy. No quarter," Tanya whispered with trepidation. She too had felt something for this white man.

"What is your obsession with spilling blood?" Thomas asked angrily and abruptly.

Papa just laughed.

"You've got a lot of your mother in you," he said smiling and patting his daughter on her knee.

"What would you propose my son?"

"I guess all we can do is release them" Thomas said matter-of-factly.

"Tend to their wounded before releasing them and pray the repercussions are minimal," Papa said. "Good night you two."

The following day was cold and blustery as April days can often be. The hospital was overflowing with army cavalry troops.

Colonel Chivington who'd been shot through the shoulder was assigned to one of the guest bedrooms in Man's house and afforded the finest of everything during his recuperation. He and Thomas were in the midst of a chess game when a rider came galloping in.

"Mr. Man. They're celebrating in the street. They say the war between the states has started in Charleston."

"And where are you coming from my good man?"

"Lawrence sir," the young rider said before turning and riding off.

"I guess we are on the same side now," Man grinned. "Now instead of fighting against your orders you are to fight on our behalf." Man laughed.

"Oh, what a difference a day makes."

"After the shellackin' we took yesterday at the hands of your troops, I too am happier to be fighting on your behalf than against you," the colonel smiled.

In all the colonel spent close to a month recuperating from his wound. Not only did he and Thomas bond around a great many things but the colonel and Papa also found a great deal to talk about.

After only a couple of weeks and thousands of deaths on both sides it soon became obvious to both sides that this call to war this would be no pushover as both sides thought going in. The North was overly confident knowing that they had two distinct advantages. They had numbers. And they were industrialized producing arms in prolific numbers.

The South on the other hand, were fighting for their livelihoods and a way of life. A way of life that they felt couldn't be and shouldn't be challenged by the federal government who they viewed as the real slave masters taking away states' rights. They too believed they had divine providence on their side. It was a sad day when the cavalry rider rode in to inform the good colonel that his stay had to be abbreviated as he was needed. Even papa and Tanya were saddened by the news of the good colonel's departure.

"Once I arrive in Washington I will address your concerns and see that the government allows you to live in peace." Colonel Chivington said hugging everyone in sight.

"And if I know anything about my friend Man here those were his intentions all along. Thomas knew that being in your company would change the entire way I viewed Coloreds. I may have had some liberal views but they were only conversational tools at dinner parties and other social gatherings. At the time it was all just ideal chat to pass the time. But after being in your company for close to a month. I must admit that all my ideal chatter about the abolition of slavery has now become my passion," the colonel admitted proudly before breaking into a broad smile. "I assume Thomas and papa had this planned from the very beginning." He said grinning broadly.

Two days later. Colonel Chivington rode east to join General Sherman in Washington. He promised to return and Maroon was left in peace.

Chapter 15

A year later the community of Maroon had once again blossomed with throngs of runaway slaves adding to the ranks. In the year after the colonel had been called away the population grew by another five thousand.

Man assigned each newcomers enough acreage to create a sizeable farm. The laws were explained in detail and taxes collected at regular intervals. The town square turned into a thriving marketplace with peddlers now coming from as far away as Texas and Missouri for various goods and services. Man's appaloosas were also a great attraction drawing a steady stream of visitors.

A church was now going up and the hospital and school were expanded. All in all the community of Maroon was thriving and everyone was prospering and doing well.

Roman Nose and Chastity Pettiway were now involved in a rather heated affair and although Roman Nose desired her greatly there was little or no chance for a committed relationship. He was the great war chief of the Southern Cheyenne and as a leader he'd long ago accepted the fact the people came first and foremost.

"Good to see you my friend," Thomas said hugging Roman Nose. "They tell me you're here all the time but I haven't seen or heard from you in a month of Sundays," Man teased knowing full well what had drawn Roman Nose's attention. An embarrassed Roman Nose was forced to smile.

"I think I've fallen for her," Roman Nose confessed dropping his head as if he'd just lost his first born son.

"Not my friend who has women of all shapes and sizes vying for his time. How many beautiful women have I seen leaving your tipi on any given day?"

"I know but this is different."

"I don't know that she's different. I just believe the way in which she brings the game to you is different."

"I'm beginning to get the feeling that you don't care too much for her."

"I wouldn't say that. I'm just leery is all. I have never really spoken to the woman long enough to even form an opinion. And aside from you I can't recall her holding a conversation with anyone."

"It really doesn't matter. The point is I like her. I like the fact that she's different from any woman I've ever met. She's cultured and knowledgeable in areas I have little knowledge of." Roman Nose said grinning like a little boy on Christmas morning.

"Well, I must say it's good to see you smile again."

"I may be smiling on the outside but inside my heart grieves."

"And what is it that causes you to grieve so my friend?"

"She says she's tired of waiting. She says she is not getting any younger and tells me she will not see me anymore until I commit to marry her."

Man dropped his head so his friend would not see him smiling.

"So, what are you going to do? It looks to me like she's pretty much spelled it out. From what I can see the writing's on the wall."

"There would be no problem but my people would never forgive me if I were to marry outside of my village. Our village has a surplus of widows on account of all the wars. The women in my village outnumber the men three-to-one. What kind of message would I be sending to the women of my village if I were to choose a woman from outside?"

"Papa always told me that the people always come before my own personal fulfillment and I suppose that it is also true in your case."

"What is it they used to tell us as children? With leadership there also comes great responsibility. Sometimes I wish I could trade it all in."

"I know the feeling my brother. Of course in Europe you sometimes have a king from one country take on a bride from another country to unite the countries. You could unite our villages in much the same way. You could use it as a purely political maneuver and expand both of our communities."

"What a mind you have my friend. That is a wonderful idea. Yes it is certainly a way to circumvent the ill will. Yes, it is a thought," Roman Nose said smiling. "You're the man!" Roman Nose said slapping his friend on the back before mounting the grey and white paint and riding off with a sense of newfound hope.

Making his daily rounds Man felt better than he had in a long time. There had been few threats on Maroon since Colonel Chivington's attack. Now everyone seemed in some way consumed by the war.

Quantrell's raiders hit Lawrence in what was called a massacre. Both Dante and Tanya were intent on hunting Quantrell down but papa did not think it prudent.

"I understand how you feel but until the president commissions us to fight I think it unwise to make this our business."

"But papa this is our business. Quantrell and his raiders are pro-slavery and against everything we are for," Tanya admonished.

"Quantrell's raiders are just one group that is pro-slavery. We cannot fight everyone whose views differ from our own. We must choose our ways to hit Quantrell without provocation or directive it would only reinforce what Southern whites already fear. And Northern whites, even the abolitionist would have second thoughts about arming Niggras. No. What I propose is to enjoy the peace and prosperity the good Lord has provided and wait patiently until President Lincoln employs us."

"I agree with papa and the way the Southern boys have been laying waste to the Union Army we should be getting the call any day now," Dante added. "Let's just bide our time for now."

Thomas waited to hear everyone before speaking.

"I just received word from Dido stating that President Lincoln's on the verge of signing the Emancipation Proclamation freeing the slaves. Dido says Niggra troops are already being employed by the army and it's just a matter of time before they will be able to bear arms."

"We've been hearing that for the past year, my husband. There are good men dying every day for our sakes, for our emancipation and even though we are armed and trained for just this sort of thing, we sit by idly while other brave men die in our stead. We sit by like old women."

"What about what papa said that you did not comprehend my wife?" Tanya who sat next to papa squeezed his hand.

"This will be the first time in the twenty summers that I've been on this earth where I can say there's been no bloodshed. And unlike you I don't particularly care for me killing another or that man trying to take my life. This is the first time and let me tell you I welcome the peace. I do not believe it was Goo's purpose to put me here solely to kill and maim," Man protested avidly "Many say I have the finest breed of horses on this side of Mississippi. Dante has six children. Papa is finally seeing and enjoying his retirement. I am sure all mentioned prefer what we are presently doing as opposed to the bloodshed that you seek, my wife."

"But if we don't fight then who? Who is better trained than we are?"

"Why do you put me in the position of having to go to some poor woman's cabin to tell her son or husband was killed in battle. No. There will be no aggressive behavior from our community. We are prospering when few are and we are doing it without help from anyone. This is what we have fought so long and hard for. We have freedom and for once peace.

How fleeting it is I don't know but let's enjoy it and continue to build from within. I'm sure we will be called to arms but until compelled to, lets enjoy this peace and prosperity God willing. There was little left to be said and that continued courtship with the idea of peace and prosperity seemed welcome by everyone – well that is except Tanya.

Later that night when they returned home the discussion returned to the war effort.

"I just don't understand why some innocent white boy like Colonel Chivington should have to die fighting my fight for my freedom when I can fight for my own freedom," Tanya shouted. "I'm not a coward."

"I totally understand that, but we are not cowards because we don't fight now. We have fought our whole lives for what has just now become a reason for them to fight. I think I will sit this one out and let someone else fight in my stead this time," Man laughed reaching for Tanya. "I can think of so many other things to do other than fight," he murmured his face now buried in her neck.

"Ooh, Man," Tanya moaned. "When you put it like that I'm inclined to agree with you," she said smiling.

The two made love until the wee hours of the morning until a rider rode in yelling.

"Quantrell's raiders hit Union troops on their way to Fort Scott. Said he massacred all the Colored troops on a second encounter at Baxter Springs. Say he killed over a hundred

U.S.Troops. That's the word coming out of Lawrence," the crier said before riding on.

"Still think our standing pat is the right choice?"

"I do until Maroon is personally threatened," Thomas said throwing on his suspenders and heading for the door.

"You going to have breakfast with me?"

"I'm afraid I can't sweetie pie. Gotta tend to the horses and check on the church construction. Those white boys helping lay the foundation are moving way too slow. Can't understand it. I'm not paying them by the hour but they act like I am. They've either got to step it up or find work elsewhere. What does your day look like?"

"Well I got Chastity Pettiway to take my classes this morning so we could spend some quality time together but it seems my husband's agenda has no room for me," Tanya said feigning hurt.

"What about tonight after work," Thomas asked.

"I'm afraid I will be working in Helen's place tonight. She sent Nat to tell me she's sick and won't be in. When I asked him what was wrong, he told me she was throwing up. I have a feeling she's pregnant again. I pray I'm wrong. We're already short staffed."

"And I'm late," he said kissing his wife. "We'll talk more when I see you tonight."

Chapter 16

An exhausted Man returned home after midnight to find Tanya sleeping soundly. Relieved he poured himself a glass of brandy and had a seat in his favorite chair in the library.

If it wasn't Mrs. Brown's cow eating Sista Gerty's petunias. It was Jeremiah promising to shoot seventeen year old Abel for sniffing around his sixteen year old daughter. If Abel had come from a family having some money for a dowry the two probably would have already been married. But the truth was Abel and his mother had barely escaped the grasp of the slave catchers and had arrived with little more than the clothes on their backs. And for that reason and that reason only did Jeremiah Johnson wanted the boy to stay away. It didn't matter that the two were in love. Fairly good with horses he had all intentions of hiring Abel to work the horses with the hopes of putting a little extra money in the young man's pockets.

This was just one of a host of local problems that Man was bombarded with on a daily basis and it was beginning to take its toll.

A knock at the door awoke him from his thoughts. "Who could it be at this hour?"

"Suh, Mr. Dante requests your company, suh."

"At this hour? What could it be son?"

"May have something to do with the army of white men at the front gate."

Thomas rode the five miles to the front gate at breakneck speed.

"What's up D?"

"You're not going to believe who is here to call on your services?"

"And who would that be?"

"White man says he needs three to four hundred fresh mounts."

"Man smiled broadly.

"Then sell them to him D. You're half-owner. Why wake me to do this business?"

"The man interested in purchasing those horses goes by the name of William. I'm sure you've heard of him. I believe he's the same man who killed the unarmed Colored soldiers a couple of days ago."

Man sat back shocked.

"So, you still wondering why I woke you, my friend?"

"Tell them we are closed for the night and will see them tomorrow."

"I already did," Dante grinned. "I figured you'd need time to mull it over although I think he has a lot of nerve to killed

199

Colored troops and then ask us for some horses so they can continue to hunt us down and kill us." Dante thought to himself aloud. "It is a lot of money though."

The reaction was no different when he arrived home.

"Is he serious," Tanya said laughing aloud. "He must really believe Colored folks ain't got no sense, no compassion for others. Damn these red neck Crackers."

These are just the type of crackers that I'd like to teach a lesson to. How many did Dante count?"

"Says there are a little more than three or four hundred."

"Which means they really pose no threat. What are you thinking?"

"That you let Quantrill and maybe three or four of his top men onto Maroon to see the horses. Then try them by military tribunal. Let justice prevail. We would be within our rights since the Union Army also wants his neck.

We garnish their assets, money, munitions and whatever valuables they may have. Once you've cut off the head the body will follow."

Man had to smile.

"I don't know why you're so devious," Man said grinning broadly now. "I swear I don't know what makes you tick but I like it. Let me run it by a couple of folks just to make sure you're not rubbing off on me. The revenues would help us greatly," he said quickly before heading back out the door.

He was certain that Dante would agree if for no more than to lift morale among the enlisted men who yearned to take part in the Union efforts if no more than to prove they were not only men but capable soldiers.

It was papa who worried him. Papa never condoned the use of violence. He always sought moderation and practiced prudence unless it threatened Maroon. And there was no way he would applaud an act of aggression against anyone regardless of their political affiliation.

Man remembers papa explaining to him after he'd been boo'ed when he let a group of captives go.

"I do not have the right to give life or take it away. That is God's job. And I do not pretend to be Him. The only job he has assigned me is to protect His children."

No, papa wasn't going to like this at all but and although he hated to go against papa's wishes it was now his call to make and he liked the idea. Quantrill's victories in both Lawrence and Baxter Springs where he massacre a hundred Colored Union soldiers made him a hero among the Confederacy. Now, Maroon's Colored troops would end Quantrill's reign of terror. They would

202

be doing their part in the war effort and perhaps would be acknowledged as the first Colored unit ready for actual battle. It appeared a win-win situation. Well, except for that he still needed to seek papa's council.

It didn't take long for papa to throw shade on the idea.

"Let me ask you this papa. We both know that I can't sell him any horses. If I refuse he will most surly attack us and attempt to take the horses by force. That will ultimately lead to too many unnecessary deaths.

What I am suggesting instead is to take Quantrill captive and his command and chase the rest away. We can turn Quantrill and his lieutenants over to the Union Army to decide his fate." Man said smiling.

This approach seemed more to papa's liking, and the two men hugged each other before Man made his leave.

Dante was more receptive and immediately called in all of his troops to get into position by morning. His plan was to encircle them leaving them no means of escape or retreat. As the night grew they would tighten the circle until they had them boxed in. Should they try or even attempt to resist it would be like duck hunting.

Man only hoped they would have the good sense to lay down their arms with the hopes of seeing another day.

Man slept alongside his lifelong friend Dante. The night was unseasonably warm and both men slept fitfully with an army behind them.

In the morning, it was the sound of horses that brought the army to attention. Quantrill and two of his officers crossed the short bridge that led to the front gate. They were followed by two men who led the covered wagon fill of gold bullion.

Once across the bridge, Man and Dante rode up to the small party of men.

"Mornin' gentlemen," Man said smiling at Quantrill.

"I ain't here to exchange pleasantries with no Niggras. I'm here to see the man who sells the horses. They say he's got a fine line of appaloosas."

"I believe I'm the man you want to see. I'm the man with the horses."

Quantrill sat there stunned. Then smiled.

"Well, I don't do business with Niggas; what will transpire now is that we will confiscate the needed mounts in the name of the war effort,"

Quantrill said calmly staring at the broad shouldered Colored man who now only obstructed his procuring the horses. "Like I said, I don't deal with niggas."

"And my husband does not do business with Southern Crackers who massacre Colored soldiers," Tanya said pulling up on her mustang.

"We will not sell you anything," she said waving her hand signaling her troops who surrounded Quantrill apprehending and taking their guns.

"What will you do with the horses we sell you? Chase down and kill more of us? I'll be damned if I let you harm another one of us or anyone else for that matter," Tanya said riding straight toward Quantrill before striking him on the temple with the butt of her rifle knocking him to the ground.

"Why you crazy ass nigga bitch!" Quantrill yelled when Man's rifle butt came smashing down knocking him unconscious. "Never mess with anyone close to Man," Dante said laughing at Man's reaction.

"How are your troops doing?" Man asked

"They're just waiting for the word."

"Well, I guess it's time we show ourselves and give them the option to surrender."

Chapter 17

"Handcuff these men," Dante ordered. "And throw them in jail for now."

Quantrill and his men were shackled at the wrists and ankles and paraded back to the front gate where he regained consciousness. Yes, there were his men, lined up along the road to the front gate milling around aimlessly, unaware that they were surrounded.

Quantrill opened his eyes to a sea of black faces.

"Everyone is in position Man," Dante reported pointing to his men on the hills as well as those on the steps of the mountain ridge and surrounding forest.

"It's now all in the hands of Mr. Quantrill here whether he wants to see his men slaughtered or live to see another day," Man replied.

Quantrill was visibly shaken as he was driven to the bridge where he yelled across to his men.

"Men there are thousands of Niggras surrounding you. And they are armed. So, what I am going to ask you all to do is to lay your guns down now and walk away from here. Go home to your families while you still can. I will call you when needed."

The men who were diehard Southern Rebels began cocking their muskets as if that were the order given. A subtle murmur could be heard. The murmur soon turned into a chorus of Dixie and call to arms could be heard. Man and Dante stared at each other in disbelief. Were these men filled with so much bitterness and hatred that would be willing to die for it?

Dante signaled his troops to stand and show themselves which they did but Quantrill's Raiders only dug in deeper.

"Take Quantrill the back way to Fort Scott then get a telegraph to Colonel Chivington and Dido that we have taken

Quantrill in custody and am transporting Quantrill to Fort Baxter,"
Man said loud enough for Quantrill's men to hear. Again there
were murmurs among the Raiders. Dante stood up on the back of
the wagon where Quantrill now sat chained.

"Those of you who have families and loved ones they
would like to see again are free to put down their weapons and
leave now," Dante shouted. He was answered with a bullet that
tore through his shirt winging his shooting arm.

"Take cover men," he said grabbing his arm and leaping
from the wagon and concealing himself in the tall, prairie grasses.

"You okay D?" Man said grabbing his friend and pulling
him inside the front gate.

"I'm good. Where's Quantrill?"

"Inside the front gate. Can you believe these men? They
must clearly know that their efforts are futile," Man said shaking
his head.

"What they know is that there is no way in hell that a Niggra is any match for a white man on a mission with God on his side. We are after all nothing more than chattel with no more smarts or intelligence than any other beast of burden but our little experiment with Maroon is exactly what Southern Crackers fear most. An independent Niggra wit' a gun. In his eyes we're his biggest threat."

"Not that we are but his own guilt make us the villain," Tanya added.

"Well, if their intent is to be martyrs and die in their attempts to do the devil's work then I will aid them in their rush to meet their maker," Dante said angrily as one of the nurses wrapped his arm.

Chapter 18

It was quiet now.

"Tell them once more," Man said praying that the Raiders would see the futility of their actions.

"Dante sent a crier in one last ditch effort to avoid the impending bloodshed.

"Go back to your homes, go back to your wives and your children. Do not make your wives widows and your children orphans." He however was not given the luxury of finishing when a barrage of shots rang out.

"I guess that's your answer Man. Now do me a favor and take Tanya and go home. I'm afraid this is not going to be pretty," Dante said assigning a small contingent to escort the two home.

"I'll send word if there are any changes," Dante said hugging both Tanya and Man before turning to direct this latest campaign.

"Well, men we have them boxed in and our numbers assure us certain victory so I want you to use discretion. Take your time and line up your target. We're in no rush. Make your shots count. Shoot to maim not to kill if at all possible. Now I want all units to advance until we have them in our crosshairs. Good luck and God bless."

An hour later, despite Dante's orders his troops who greatly outnumbers Quantrill's Raiders still hadn't advanced. The leaderless Raiders weren't used to losing and fought valiantly and with much heart. Agonizing screams denoting pinpoint accuracy could be heard from both camps and Maroon's superior forces were somehow kept at bay.

No more than an hour later Helen jumped down from her horse and found her husband standing on the edge of the bluff overlooking the battle region.

"This shouldn't be D. No way should it take this long to do away with such a small force." Helen acknowledge almost as if she were stating the length of time it took to make one of her infamous lemon meringue pies.

"I now know why I married you," Dante quipped sarcastically. "It was obviously for your hindsight and clear perception," he grinned. "What pray tell would you have me do?"

"Send the girls in, at least the snipers to knock out both Gatling guns. Send one unit in specifically to silence the howitzers and cannons. Their artillery is what's killing us."

"If that's how you see it then make that call Helen."

Turning on her heels Helen stomped away, entered the command tent and gave the orders before returning to her

215

husband's side. The two were alone now except for Dante's personal security.

"May I have a word with my husband," Helen queried as she took notice of the guards as she entered the command post. The four men acknowledging her request exited the tent.

Helen made her way across to Dante and had a seat opposite of him. Taking his hands in hers she stared deeply into his eyes before placing her lips on his, kissing him deeply, passionately. Reaching for her she pushed him away.

"Perhaps tonight, but we have more pressing issues at present."

"Then what was that for?"

"I just wanted you to know how much I love you."

"I'm not quite sure I understand. Can we try that again," he grinned.

"My point exactly. You're a good man Dante. I couldn't have asked for more in a mate. You're compassionate and that's one of the primary reasons I married you but your compassion at times like these is becoming a problem. This should have been over a long time ago D. Your indecisiveness in ending this is causing us more casualties than is necessary. It's almost as if you're waiting for those Crackers to pack up and head home.

What you're failing to understand is that they're so full of hatred that they'd rather die than to relinquish their beliefs to a bunch of niggas. In their heads they cannot and will not be defeated by a bunch of ignorant, heathen, runaway slaves.

It's time to put all reason and compassion away and take these Crackers out before we lose another man."

Dante dropped his head.

"You know me too well, my wife," Dante said before getting up and taking her into his arms.

217

Minutes later Dante exited the tent where he was quickly updated on his troops.

"Suh, we were unable to take the Gatling or the canons."

"Any causalities?"

"Nineteen deaths. Twelve wounded suh. They're dug in pretty well sir and they don't look to be going anywhere. Seem to me like they're in it for the long run suh."

Dante thought about his wife's words before speaking. Hard as it was to admit she was right these men were fighting men. That was all they knew. He didn't even think about the cause mattered but if there were any incentive it was the fact that the world was in chaos when niggas took up arms against white folks. Now his scouts had confirmed it.

"Tell Ms. Helen to stand by. Once we flush them out, tell them to have her snipers ready."

"Yes, sir," the young said riding off.

Dante turned to his lieutenants.

"Let's put an end to this now. I want you to attack both flanks on my command. I will lead the frontal attack. Be aware the Quantrill's forces don't fight in the traditional way the Calvary does but will resort to guerrilla warfare in much the same way the Cherokees do. What we will probably see is them dig in even deeper or take to the trees."

"They were given the opportunity to walk away. They chose not to. Whatever their reasons are I cannot allow them anymore success. They must be stopped now. Tell your men to keep their heads down. These men are crack shots. You will attack on my signal. Now move out."

The men moved out under Dante's command. When the signal was given the 1st and 2nd battalions let loose a steady barrage on Q's men. But and despite the assault by Dante's troops the Raiders could not be dislodged.

"Looks like this may be a war of attrition," Dante said two days later at the council meet. "We've hit them with everything we have and they seem to be unaffected. And their Gatling won't allow us to advance.

"Is there a need to advance? We have their entrance and exit cut off. And it's only a matter of time before their rations begin to run out. There's no need for any more casualties at this point. Just sit tight and monitor their behavior. They may reconsider our offer when their bellies grow hungry," Man said.

"Then it is simply a matter of waiting them out then?"

"Yes, my friend. Let Helen's sharpshooters keep them pinned down and just keep watch. Hunger will take the fight out of the best men. Other than that, I have nothing else."

Chapter 19

Tanya stood.

"Dido will be home this week after being away the last two months in Washington doing our bidding. Make sure that he's welcomed home appropriately."

"I would assume that would be Umi's job," Helen said smiling mischievously.

"And that's why you have six children," Tanya laughed.

"And working on seven," Helen laughed. "You know what they say. Practice makes perfect."

A week later, a white flag rose and a tall, white man sporting a thick beard came in. The man rode in alone while Dante and Tanya sat across from each other, a chess game loomed large between them.

"Checkmate!" Tanya yelled as the messenger walked in.

"Suh, one of dem Raiders is here under a white flag," the young man said.

"Thank you son."

Stepping into the warm night air it soon became apparent that Man's prognostication was coming true.

"Yes suh. What can I do for you?" Dante asked.

"Nigga, we need water. My men…"

The sound of the .45 colt revolver ended the man's sentence.

"And why we would give you anything? You kill my people and then you demand my assistance so you can continue to maim and kill me and mine. No sir. I won't let that happen," Tanya said before emptying her revolver into the man's already limp figure.

Dante stood there shaken.

"Tee..."was all that he could muster.

But it was Helen who stood by watching who picked up the mantle.

"When the 1st battalion is in position fire one shot. When I fire back I want you to hit them with everything we have and I want my unit to concentrate your fire on their big guns. Is that understood?"

Members of the 1st rode away.

"No quarter, no mercy," yelled Tanya as the troops rallied for their latest assault.

Chapter 20

A shaken Dante said nothing. What could he say? He was a man of peace and would have given anything to see that there was no more blood spilled on this day but his sentiments were obviously not shared. He realized that the hatred between Colored and white folks had been born upon the capture and enslavement of the first African to land in this land but he felt in no way bitter nor would he allow it to hold him hostage.

No, if he were to truly be free then he couldn't be held captive by a need to do another man harm. All that he asked was to be left alone to farm his land, provide for his ever-growing family, and raise his horses. That was all he wanted.

He never wanted to be responsible for the giving or talking of another man's life be he white or Black. What had papa always said? When it came to decreeing whether or not a man was to live or die? I am not God.

Dante thought of all this and more as the sound of gun fie rang out like thunder in the distance.

Man rode in a broad smile etched up his face.

"Dido's home," he shouted. "He brings us good news from the nation's capital," he said looking at his friend and immediately knowing that something was wrong.

"Talk to me brother."

Dante recalled earlier events including Quantrill's man being shot down under a white flag.

"Granted he should have never rode in sayin' and demandin' niggas to do this and that but we all know that he was under the protection of the white flag when there's no doubt that they were in the process of surrendering. Now they are in the process of being slaughtered, without my consent."

Man dropped his head before summoning one of Dante's guards.

"See here man. Go to Ms. Helen and tell her to allow what's left of Quantrill's raiders to go free."

"Yas suh," the young lieutenant said snapping off a salute before turning and heading for his horse.

"C'mon D. I think the girls can wrap things up. Let's go see Dido."

The two rode miles before a word was uttered.

"Do you recall my asking you why Tanya seemed to have such an affinity for killing?"

"I do."

"Today you're in a state of shock because you got to witness it first hand and it's not sitting well with you. The fact of the matter is that this all falls back on you my friend," Man said smiling broadly again.

"How is that?" Dante cried.

"Well, if I'm not mistaken I believe it was you who decreed that Tanya was to relinquish her position and was not to be allowed to be engage in combat. She is in clear violation of the law and needs to be apprehended and brought before the council on charges," Man said, the smile gone now.

"You're not serious?" Dante said searching his friend's face for answers.

"You'd be doing us both a favor. Send a man back to have her arrested as soon as the Quantrill's men are released."

"You're serious?"

"What kind of signal would we be sending the people of Maroon if our chief law enforcement officer is allowed to break the law at her whim? And don't worry about any repercussions. I'll handle that."

"And you think we were just in a battle?" Dante laughed. "She's going to be hot as a wet hen. I wouldn't want to be in your shoes when she's released."

That very evening the house was full of laughter and good conversation. Tanya jumped down from her horse and ran up the steps, kissed Thomas on the cheek, nodded at Dante before hitting the door.

"Where's Dido?"

"I'm in the library, T," Dido yelled back.

Chapter 21

Man turned to Dante.

"I thought we agreed..." Man whispered.

"Didn't want to embarrass her in front of the troops she'd just led to victory. Told them to wait till after dinner."

"Guess that makes sense. C'mon. I can't wait to hear how we were received in Washington."

Man nor anyone else were disappointed in Dido's recollection.

"It took me two weeks before I could even get an audience. It wasn't until Colonel Chivington spoke on our behalf that I was even given an audience. In any case, they condoned our being here and because of the war we are not responsible to local government who we do not hold our allegiance to. Instead we are under the direct authority of the federal government who we hold our allegiance to. And although we have no representation as of yet we still present a viable force. And they are courting our votes even before we have been given the right to vote. Yet, they know it is coming. However, even at present, if we can get enough signatures we can send a representative to Congress with our needs and concerns.

Currently we have the right to defend ourselves. That is an inherent right. Any aggressive acts will be prosecuted to the full extent of the law and once President Lincoln allows Colored soldiers to bear arms we will be duly employed in the war effort in combat situations. But here's the kicker our battalions will be recruited but will remain in intact although I am sure that the man the top will be white. This was all due to Chivington's glowing appraisal of our armed forces.

I'm trying to lobby to get Chivington placed in charge since they insist on having a white man to lead our troops." Dido was saying before Tanya was called to the front door. Helen stood there.

"I'm sorry T. I was on-duty when I received the order to place you under arrest."

Helen placed the cuffs on her friend ever so gently.

"Man!"

Both Man and Dante appeared as well as papa curious to see what all the commotion was about.

"I know one of you is responsible for this," Tanya said smiling.

"I'm sorry T but you broke the law twice today. You killed a man in cold blood who was under a white flag of truce and then you took part in a battle knowing full well that you have been admonished from all combat. You will be tried and sentenced following your trial tomorrow. Until then you are remanded to your jail." Dante said rather matter-of-factly.

"And what does my husband have to say concerning these allegations?" T said grinning. There was a coldness in her eyes Man had seen only once or twice.

"I must concur with Dante. We have instilled the laws and have to realize that even though my wife is the one being prosecuted by the law that there is no one who is above the law," Man said before taking Tanya in his arms and hugging her tightly.

Helen led T down the steps and to the wagon where she was loaded and taken to jail.

Man was the first to approach the jail in the morning.

"Good morning m'love," he said smiling and handing her the freshly picked daisies.

"How could you? What was on your mind? I mean really Man. What man has his own wife arrested and jailed. The next thing you'll be telling me is how much you love me…"

"I do love you. This has nothing to do with my feeling towards you."

"Well, that's obvious," she said throwing the vase of daisies at him. Water, shattered glass and daisies now covered the floor of the tiny cell. It was obvious by this point that there was no talking, no reasoning with her.

"The trial's to be held at noon. I will see you then T," Man said exiting the jail to a chorus of curses.

Dante was already in the corral working his horses when Thomas rode us.

"How's she farin'?"

"Not too good. She's mad as a wet hen and of course I'm to blame"

"Of course."

"Even papa said I may have been too harsh but he agreed that she needs to be held accountable."

"There you go. One thing you can always count on with papa. Love you or hate you papa's gonna tell you the hard truth."

"That may be true but he never told me how hard this marriage thing is."

Dante laughed.

"He may not have had a partner quite like yours. T is one of a kind. She's definitely a challenge… even for you. And my sorrow already goes out to you should the council do anything more than give her a slap on the wrist," Dante grinned. "I'm just glad I'm not in your shoes my brother."

A slap on the wrist and a stern warning was all she received and a week later Tanya still hadn't uttered a word to him or anyone else.

"I won't be coming home tonight. Seems Helen is pregnant again and can't assume her duties."

Man heard the door slam and breathed a sigh of relief. The week had really tested his resolve. It had started off with Roman Nose approaching him. Only this time it wasn't about the comely Miss Pettiway but his Man's tendency to be too soft, too compassionate in warfare.

Seems the Quantrill men he'd released had somehow resurfaced not long after their attack on Maroon to massacre a small band of Cherokees, some forty miles west. Perhaps Tanya had been right in her disdain for those same men who went on to murder some sixty women and children. He'd followed his conscience and his faith to preserve life and how had these white men repaid his benevolence? By murdering innocent women and children. Had these men no souls? Now he was forced to carry the weight of their transgressions. It was times like these when he questioned what papa referred to as his blessing, birthright, and curse. And now Tanya was angry with him. He couldn't seem to win for losing.

All in all, Maroon was thriving. Dante and Helen were expecting their seventh child any day now. Papa had channeled his energies into teaching all the young men in the village their history.

Tanya had finally returned to her old self, playful, in love and as always very supportive of her husband but something was different.

These days Man saw little of his wife. She was still acting as maroon's Chief Constable, primary teacher as well as covering for Helen who was in the last few weeks of her pregnancy while community matters kept him busy. He hardly had time for his horses and if it weren't for Dante he would have lost the herd.

"Looks like you have everything in order. I'm proud of you son. You've certainly moved us to the next level. Now it's time to put her fate in the hands of the people. Arrange an election, and have them elect a government and lessen the stress and workload on yourselves. Then you can do what you really love to do, raise appaloosas, and make us all rich. And then if you can ever slow that woman of yours down perhaps you can make me a grandfather." Papa smiled broadly.

He'd had the same thoughts but lately either or both had been too exhausted. Papa was right. They really should start delegating duties. Thomas considered peeking in on T and perhaps even accompanying her while she made her rounds. It was a cool enough night and it was always quiet in Maroon. The only thing open this time of night was the inn and soup kitchen that welcomed runaways at any time of day or night.

No. She'd be fine he thought to himself as he made his way up the spiral staircase to the master bedroom where he picked up de Tocqueville's Democracy in America. Minutes later he was snoring softly the book resting on his chest.

Chapter 22

"Hey hon. You asleep?" Tanya yelled as she placed the chocolate cake and pork shoulder on the kitchen table. "Miss Mae sent you some ham for your breakfast. I swear that woman's got a crush on you and it don't seem to matter that you have a wife or not," T teased.

"Here you go again. You know Miss Mae's old enough to be my mother and she ain't thinkin' 'bout me. She just knows I like good food."

"She and Chastity Pettiway are about the same age ain't they?"

"And your point?"

"Well, you and Roman Nose are the same age and he doesn't seem to mind a woman a few years older."

"To each his own I suppose. But me, personally I'm quite satisfied with my non-cooking wife," Man said grabbing T and nuzzling her neck.

"Behave yourself sir. I need to grab a quick nap before I go in to see my children in the morning," T grinned.

"You know papa and I were just talking about that…"

"Talking about…"

"We were talking and we agreed that we are doing a wonderful job but we need to scale back and start delegating a lot of the workload. He seems to think that we are killing ourselves and I tend to agree. And especially where you're concerned."

Tanya did not reply.

"I think we have enough in the treasury to hire a full time teacher. And I'd appreciate it if you'd look into that for me." Man said his smile gone now.

Seeing he was serious she agreed.

"I'll do that in the morning. I have to admit that last night was kind of rough. Let me see if I can't get a couple of hours of shut eye before I have to go in," T kissed him on the cheek before heading to bed.

In the morning Man grabbed his coat and headed to the corral where Nat, Dante and Roman Nose were hard at work breaking a young mustang.

"What's the good word family?"

Dante's oldest, Nat was no novice when it came to horses and soon had the mustang under his control. Dismounting he turned to Man.

"Hey unk. Today's my birthday."

"I know I believe I was there when you were born," Man said before taking his arm from behind his back and placing a rather large, gift-wrapped package in the boy's arms.

The weight of the package was so heavy the boy fell to the ground when Man handed it to him as everyone laughed.

"Ah thanks Uncle Thomas," the elated young man shouted.

"I don't believe I got the same reaction when I handed him my gift," Roman Nose quipped.

"Show Man what Roman Nose gave you," Dante prodded his son.

"Ah, Uncle Rome made this for me," the boy said holding up an exquisitely carved pipe.

"Very nice," Thomas said examining the pipe closely. "You ought to consider putting a few of these in the general store. You could probably make a pretty penny off of these."

"Takes too much time. Besides these are only for those close to me."

"I gotcha," Man said smiling and watching as the young boy tore the paper off his gift before yelling.

"Ahh... Thanks unk," he said grabbing the hand carved saddle and throwing it on the young stallion.

"The stallions yours too. It comes from all three of us," Man said.

"I got the best damn family of any boy in Maroon, "Nat said grinning from ear-to-ear. "And I thank you all. But I still have one request," Nat said sheepishly.

"After all that?" Dante groaned.

"Let the boy talk D." Roman Nose added.

"The legal age for a boy to enlist in the army is sixteen. Well, being that I'm sixteen can I enlist?"

All three men dropped their heads.

"Well, can I?"

All eyes were on D now who after having seen more than his share of bloodshed was reluctant.

"Let's leave that decision up to your mother," D said passing the buck. "She may have other plans for you. Now come on we have more work to do before that mid-day sun hits."

It was then that Roman Nose pulled Ned to the side of the corral.

"Be careful of what you wish for Nat," was all any of the men could muster. "The way they've been raiding the border it may not be long before you may be called to enter the madness."

"I'm ready," Nat replied. "I can already ride and shoot with the best of them. I'm just wasting my time going to school."

"Don't rush it son. Shooting a man is not like shooting a deer. It's something that you never get over."

All three men nodded with grave faces.

"The border raids are growing more frequent now and are getting closer and closer to Maroon. My braves have already had three or four encounters with these men. They claim they're pro-slavery and fight for the Confederates but what they really are poor, white, dirt farmers who see robbing and killing the less fortunate as lucrative," Roman Nose said to all but no one in particular.

"How serious is it?"

"If I were you Man, I'd extend your perimeter guard and add some more scouts."

"That bad?"

"Won't be long before they're knockin' on your doorstep. They don't number enough to be any real threat but if they catch you off guard the lives of your women and children will be on your conscience."

"We'll be ready for them when they come. Won't we papa?" Nat shouted.

"Yes, we'll be ready son."

"One more thing. These men don't fight in the traditional sense. They're led by Bloody Bill and its obvious Cherokees trained him. He employs guerilla tactics, guerilla warfare to advance his cause."

"Good to know. Thank you my brother," Dante said hugging his friend.

"They'll most likely be coming for the horses. Everyone west of the Mississippi knows you have the finest mounts around."

"Thanks for the heads up my friend. By the way, how are you and Miss Pettiway doing? I haven't heard you speak of her lately." Man teased lightheartedly hoping to bring some levity to the situation.

"I really couldn't tell you. She refuses to see me but still sends me a plate on occasion just to remind of what I'm missing. But she still won't allow me to see her," Roman Nose said dejectedly.

"Still no plans to tie the knot?" Dante interjected.

"What is it they say? Misery loves company," Roman Nose teased halfheartedly.

"I'm content if not happy," Dante countered.

"So am I," Thomas added although he'd spent the last two weeks trying to figure out he could improve his marriage. There were really no glaring or insurmountable problems. He and Tanya still had a tremendous amount of love for each other but saw less and less of each in lieu of their communal responsibilities.

Man often thought that Tanya took her duties even more seriously than he. And now since Helen was pregnant she worked even harder trying to fill both her duties as well as Helens. Thomas couldn't remember the last time they shared a bed or night together.

No this working nights had to end especially if he were to give papa those grand babies he so longer for.

That day he confronted Tanya.

"Baby, we've finally found us a home. And with the herd growing the way it is I can honestly say that we are better off than we've ever dreamed," he said hugging T and whispering in her ear.

"You are absolutely right and the people are prospering as well. Now tell me my husband. What brings this on?"

"The fact that I don't get to share my bed with my wife bothers me. I want you to get someone to replace Helen."

T let his words sink in and took her time responding.

"If Maroon has any problems of concerns it usually happens at night during Helen's shift."

"What kinds of problems?"

"Oh, you know. Drunk and disorderly. Fights, domestic violence that sort of thing," Tanya said.

"And you can't find some able-bodied person to do the job?"

"I just found a teacher to replace me, but give me some time. I promise you this won't last forever. Give me a few weeks," Tanya said nuzzling his neck with her nose. "I'm training Diola to take my place. I think she'll make a fine sergeant of arms."

A week later, Dante met Thomas at the local watering hole.

"Give me a cold one, Lucas." Dante said flipping the gold piece at the bartender. "You know it's a funny thing Thomas. Roman Nose's scouting reports have all been precise and on point. The pro-slavery forces are conducting border raids all around us but for some reason have avoided Maroon. It's the strangest thing"

"What is it they say? Don't look a gift horse in the mouth."

"I guess you're right but it's almost as if we are being watched over and protected."

"Perhaps you're right. God looks out for his children you know and there is no way we would have made it this far without His guidance and protection. I firmly believe that." Man replied, sipping his beer not making much of the small talk. But D. was right. God was obviously watching over them.

And then the word came. President Lincoln had freed the slaves and finally allowed Colored troops the right to fight. It was almost as if God the father had taken time to personally bless them and finally taken them out of Babylon.

The air in Maroon was now full of hopeful optimism. For everyone knew that if the former slaves had any parts of confronting their formers masters it was just a matter of time before the war for freedom would be over.

Not a week later Man received a telegraph from Dido in Washington stating that Maroon's armed forces were commissioned to join the war effort and would remain intact under Colonel Chivington's command and at my behest he would be honored to take the position. Dido thought this better than having a stranger assigned to our plight. Chivington would arrive within the coming weeks.

"Would you like that I stay here or may I return to my beloved Umi who I miss dearly?' Signed, your friend and brother, Dido."

The news came as no surprise to anybody aside from Umi who was thrilled that her man was finally coming home.

Within the month Major Chivington and Dido arrived at Maroon. The reunion was a joyful occasion for everyone especially Umi, a large black woman, the color of midnight with distinct African features. No one could be more ecstatic. Dido had come to know Umi days after her arrival in Maroon. As with all arriving runaways Mama assigned her a sponsor and a tutor to help make their transition much smoother.

Dido, who'd been educated much in the same manner as Man and Tanya had shown an inclination to scholarly pursuits and a voracious appetite for the written word was quickly assigned the role of tutor for all newly arrived runaways. Dido reveled in this capacity but when it came to Umi he worked painstakingly hard to make sure she received all the knowledge he had to give.

Fifteen years earlier she'd arrived in Charleston like so many others as a slave and captive but the fire within her refused to allow her to be broken and she and another woman know as Lucy had both vowed to escape even before they disembarked the slave ship.

Once told, how they were to be shipped once again to be sold to work the snake and mosquito laden waters of the rice plantations and serve her new masters it was said that Umi commented 'I have one master and his name is Allah.'

The ship's captain hearing this summarily had her whipped. Two days later with no idea of where they were going Umi and Lucy escaped before ever seeing the auction block. But what most attracted Dido was the young woman's voracious appetite for learning that propelled Dido to achieve even greater academic endeavors.

And it was Umi who in her man's departure from Maroon had commissioned Man to fund her enough monies to build Maroon's first library which was simply and extension of Dido's own personal collection which consisted primarily of two roomfuls of military and historical volumes.

In the six months that Dido had been in Washington, Umi who was a member of Maroon's welcoming committee saw that every visitor in spite of their reasons for visiting Maroon whether it be to purchase corn, potatoes or horses, add to the library's collection. Within the six months Dido had been gone Umi had grown the library from a paltry two rooms to an excess of six rooms with volumes coming in regularly.

Even Colonel Chivington, a voracious reader in his own right had to comment that the library could rival those of the best of New England's personal libraries.

When the festivities surrounding the two men's arrival including food and libations was over Umi grabbed Dido's hand made their farewells and led him not to the bedroom, as one would think after such a long absence as this but to the newly expanded library. Umi was not at all surprised at Dido's reaction since they'd discussed the importance of creating a library. He was thrilled.

"They don't want us to learn to read, write or be literate," Umi had commented when they'd first discussed the idea before his leaving.

"The law specifically forbids Colored slaves from learning or being taught to read. And there is good reason for that. As long as he can keep us blind and in the darkness he can keep us in the dark and teach us what to believe.

Over the past year or so I have read his King James Bible twice and I still cannot find where is says that Africans should be servant to the European. That I cannot find and doubt that I ever will. It is up to us to bring our people out of the darkness and enlighten them."

Dido could do little but smile and acknowledge Umi's words at the time but he'd never expected anything of this magnitude on his return. He beamed with pride knowing the he'd done as much as anyone in the colony shape this woman's mindset.

Still, her intent, desire, and motivation arose from within and her African heritage. And here he was looking at the very clear and real culmination of her work. So, enthralled and enchanted was he by Umi's work that after holding her in his arms until she was gasping for breath he fell to his knees and looking up into her beautiful, brown eyes and murmured the words.

"Will you do me the honor of being my wife, my Umi?" He said almost pleading.

Umi who was playful by her very nature smiled at the six foot six mound of muscle before her.

"You know I will my love but according to custom you must first ask my father. Then you must seek to pay him a dowry for my hand. In my country, this can be done with cattle, horses or something else as a token of my worth," Umi said looking quite serious.

"But Umi, your father is in Africa," Dido replied almost brokenhearted by her response.

"Well, then I suggest you start working on your passage," she replied before breaking into a large grin.

"Oh, woman you had me going there for a while," Dido said before standing and hugging her once again.

"Seriously though I think we need to talk about your upcoming plans. With Maroon entering the war I sense that you my love will want to do your part and will be off with the first call to arms. And I'm sure there will be much grief and sorrow here in Maroon in the next few months. I don't want to be married only to be made a widow. And I don't want to be sitting here while my husband lobbies for Maroon's interest in Washington," Umi, said. There was little or no humor in her voice now. "You know as well as I do that the interests of the colony come before the personal needs of the individual."

Dido dropped his head knowing that she was correct in her observations.

"Tomorrow evening the inner council meets to discuss that very thing and I can almost assure you that not every men will take part in the war effort. I'm almost certain that those men who opt to fight will join on a voluntary basis and those men that have families or have civic responsibilities will not be allowed to fight.

If Man decides that I need to return to Washington then you will be by my side. Either way we will be together as husband and wife." Dido said now showering Umi with warm kisses.

"Sounds delightful," Umi said but the smile, which was so apart of her daily make up was gone.

"What is it my love?"

"I do not believe from the letters you have sent me that Washington D.C. is hardly my type of life Dido. Yes, it sounds glamorous in your depictions. But I have, like you my love, carved out my own niche right here in Maroon. I have taken over for Tanya as lead teacher in the Norman School and the construction and maintenance of the library fulfills me. Besides what would I do in D.C.? I am if nothing else little more than a chubby lil' country gal."

"No, Umi. You are so much more than that. Yes, my love you are so much more than that. At least to me you are. You are just what our nation capital needs. I see women every day at their prestigious, little teas but I have not as of yet met a woman with your substance. They are hardly in your league my dear."

"And perhaps that's why I love you so much you silver-tonged devil you," Umi said laughing now in hopes of making light of the whole affair.

"But seriously though, you are by your very nature an earth shaker, a thinker, a mover of men so do your duty and I will be here when the dust settles."

A much dejected Dido leaned back in the Queen Ann chair while Umi approached kissing him on his forehead affectionately and placing a leather bound volume in his lap.

"You made mention of this when I last saw you. I had to search far and wide but was finally able to procure a copy," she said handing him a rather worn copy of de Tocqueville's Democracy in America.

"I must admit it is a most entertaining read."

All Dido could do was smile.

Chapter 23

Colonel Chivington was exhausted from his trip. It had taken well over a month to make the journey from the nation's capital to Maroon and with the relatively new Fugitive Slave Act being rigorously enforced it wasn't safe for Coloreds travelling let alone a white New Englander posing to be a Southern planter. If there was one thing the Rebs hated more than a runaway slave, it was those New England abolitionists intent on destroying their southern tradition and way of life.

There had been several close calls along the way but none had been any closer than the last which occurred only twenty or so miles outside of Maroon where pro-slavery men had stopped them

"Say there suh, please state the nature of your business," the red headed gentle who appeared to be in charge inquired.

"Well suh, from what I've been told there's a man in these here parts that breeds some of the finest horse flesh around."

"Say boy you don't sound like you from these here parts. Sounds more to me like you got some Yankee in you."

"You are correct my good man, my mama's from Massachusetts but my daddy's from Louisiana. My mama sent me back North when I was knee high to a grasshopper to get what she considered a quality education. But anyway, and if you don't mind me asking, what is all this about gentleman?"

"Say boy, I believe we're asking the questions here. Now please tell me what this here niggas gots to do with anything? And has you got the proper papers sayin' the niggas yours?"

"I do suh," the colonel said reaching into his pocket at which time all four of the gentleman on horseback cocked their firearms.

"Whoa, whoa gentleman. There's certainly no need for that." Colonel Chivington said handing over the paper work when a rider rode up.

"And please explain

"Why do you have this here nigga with you?"

"Well suh. This here boy is one of daddy's finest niggas and was apprehended in Delaware. Papa sent me to fetch him back and from I've been told the man selling the horses is said to be a nigga. I figures he'd have a better chance of getting' a fair deal than I would. Being that they speaks the same language," the colonel said smiling broadly.

It was obvious that the four men on horseback were more than a little leery when the rider who had just pulled up began to speak.

"Suh, they just attacked the camp!"

267

"Who attacked the camp?" yelled the leader.

"Can't rightly say, suh. They were dressed in all black with black hoods. Ol' John said from what he could see they 'peared to be niggas. Whoever they was they was crack shots. June boy and four others is dead."

"Ol' John bout senile. Y'all know well as I do that ain't no nigga in their right mind gonna attack a camp like ours especially without some white man behind them. It's either the abolitionist or some kin to John Brown if niggas is involved."

"C'mon let's go!" The burly, red haired man said before wheeling his horse around and riding off.

Both Dido and the colonel knew that they remained alive only by the grace of God.

Colonel Chivington who by now had come close to death more times than he cared to remember awoke in Maroon around mid-day the following day and fell to his knees immediately.

By this time, he was well aware that his most recent undertaking was frowned upon by not only his fellow officers but by the South as well who decreed that any Union officer in command of Colored troops would be outside of the general rules of warfare and would summarily be hung for their involvement with Colored contraband.

Still, it was his mother who said to him upon his leaving that a man who had any grit or sand in him should not be afraid to live or die for what he believed in. His thoughts were interrupted by a knock.

"Suh," the young pretty dark-skinned maiden said smiling. "Would you like to take lunch in your quarters or be served at the council meeting which begins in half-an-hour?"

"Is it possible that I could eat after the meeting? I'm still plumb full from that feast we had last night."

"As you wish sir," she said before closing the door and making her leave.

Twenty minutes later, Colonel Chivington made his way down the long, spiral staircase and into the parlor where dozens of Maroon citizens sat in eager anticipation of what was to come. It was Man who spoke first.

"First of all, I'd like to welcome my good friend Colonel Chivington here today. Most of you already know that the good colonel has agreed to lead our armies in the war for our freedom."

A loud cheer went up throughout the room.

"Thank you. Thank you. Not more than a year ago I had to my displeasure of fighting against your army and I must say that in my twelve years as an officer I have not fought against a better equipped or well-trained army. So, it is my honor to be able to lead them at this time."

"No disrespect colonel but if that is the case then why does President Lincoln insist on you leading our forces when those same forces defeated you armies? Seems to me that if anything he would have Dante or Man leading your armies," Tanya said, leaving the room stunned. Papa dropped his head. The old man couldn't help but smile.

"Tanya!" Man shouted.

"No, Man," the colonel interrupted. "Tanya is well within her rights to ask and though it is well beyond my rank and pay grade it is a legitimate question so let me see if I can answer. Yes, the last time we met your army soundly thrashed us. That was a year ago. Since then President Lincoln has done everything to preserve the State-of-the-Union despite the South's intent to see it crumble.

Now should we win this war, and we will, there will be some healing that must take place. If Lincoln is to do this he cannot exacerbate the existing wounds. And he has already done that by freeing the slaves and by implanting General Order number 143 allowing Coloreds to bear arms against those very same people who previously owned them is tantamount to heresy or treason among Southern whites.

So, you see if President Lincoln has any chance at all of healing the nation when this war is over he must be very careful on how he proceeds moving forward. As for me, I am no more than a figurehead. What papa, Man, and Dante have accomplished can hardly be undermined and when the fighting begins I will be no more than concerned onlooker. Are there any more questions?"

There were no more and Man made it clear that any man having two or more children twelve years of age or younger would not be allowed to participate in the war effort. That was other than Dante who was given the title of general and who also relegated to the rear along with Colonel Chivington. The women's contingent was also not allowed to participate.

In all, more than three brigades, close to ten thousand men were employed under General Dante's command as well as more than two hundred of Roman Nose's braves who volunteered as scouts.

Two brigades of close to six thousand men were left to defend the home front which by now was quite fortified with foxholes, stone walls and bridges put firmly in place to prevent any unwanted visitor's advances.

When all was quiet it was decided that the colonel and Dante's army would move out within the week and much to his surprise Dido would command the home forces. Along with Roman Nose's Cheyenne village which made camp right outside of the gates of Maroon, it was almost impenetrable.

It was a sad day when the soldiers left leaving many a wife or girlfriend in tears. One who wasn't was Chasity Pettiway who was having quite a hard time with Roman Nose in such close proximity.

"Okay, chief I guess I can understand your allegiance and your loyalty to your people and since I cannot have you all to myself I will take what you have to offer," she whispered barely loud enough for him to hear.

"Then it is settled," Roman Nose smiled his heart content. "As is the custom of my people I will make you my fourth and final wife. We will have many sons, my wife but first I must go down to Mexico and deliver these horses for my brother Thomas. I shan't be gone more than a couple of moons."

"Oh, baby, can't you send some of your trusted braves? Do you know how long I've waited for you?"

"My friend has entrusted me with this mission. I am to bring back five thousand head of Texas Longhorns to make sure Maroon is supplied next winter. He's depending on me."

"Then I will go with you," the very attractive and voluptuous Ms. Pettiway replied.

Roman Nose was forced to smile.

"The trail is long and hard and no place for a woman of your stature. But should you choose to go I would be glad to have you accompany me," Roman Nose chimed.

"Then it's settled," Chastity beamed.

"We leave on the next full moon," Roman Nose said wheeling his horse in and grinning from cheek-to-cheek.

"But first we will be married. On the fortnight my love." She said pulling him over to kiss him before he rode off.

If there was anyone more elated than Chastity Pettiway that night it was Umi who was absolutely thrilled that Dido had been relegated to Commander and Chief of the home forces.

That Saturday, along with Umi, Dido, Chastity and Roman Nose, Tanya and Man sat down to dinner with some of their closest friends.

"So, it's agreed then. This Saturday we will have a dual wedding for our dearest friends," Tanya said making a toast to everyone seated.

"It's agreed then!" Man said lifting his glass before walking around the table hugging everyone and filling the glasses with more brandy.

"It's a good day for everyone." Roman Nose said before making his leave. The rest of the party made their way towards the front door. Upon opening it came the quick succession of gunfire.

In came a rider. It was Dante's oldest Nat who'd quickly risen to the rank of 2nd lieutenant

"Uncle Dido, Uncle Man. Confederate soldiers and I mean there are a lot of 'em. Must be more than a thousand of 'em. More than I've ever seen before. And they're led by someone named General Nathan Bedford Forest. Seems they've been scouting us for weeks now and watched as papa and the colonel pulled out."

"You did well son. Send word for the rest of the men to dig in and get word to the reserves to join us at the front," Dido instructed.

"And I thought you going off to fight would be even more dangerous. Is there no place that's safe for Niggras?" Umi said dejectedly.

"Nowhere I've ever been in this man's America." Tanya said strapping on her sidearm.

"I do believe we've already been through this T. You're not to take part in the actual fighting." Man commanded.

"But if it's as many as the boy said you're gonna need every gun you can get."

"Let's see if we can't get a closer look before you take to the front?" Dido said summoning both Roman Nose and Man.

By the time they reached the front gate Roman Nose's scouts were already on the inside and waiting on his arrival.

"Many, many grey coats with heavy artillery. Too many to fight head-to-head. From what I can see they outnumber us at least three-to-one.

"They may outnumber us but we are impenetrable and can win a war of attrition. Your braves can make it virtually impossible for them to get supplies in or out and our snipers can keep them pinned down for as long as you like," Dido commented to Man.

"I cannot commit Roman Nose's troops to our fight," Man remarked. "And like I was saying, since you've been gone T and her unit have been forbidden from engaging in any skirmishes or battles."

"My brother's enemies are my enemies," Roman Nose said coming to his friend's aid. "It was you who took in our children and our old and fed them when they were on the verge of starving last winter. This is no longer simply your fight my brother. This is our fight."

Man could do little more than smile.

"And I promise we will stay out of range my husband but let the women do what they do best. I promise we'll stay on the bluff. We'll simply concentrate on taking their artillery out of play," T said nuzzling her husband's neck until he had no choice but to concede.

"Man?" Dido said waiting for the go ahead.

"Summon Helen and the girls," Man said. "And let's get this done."

Less than an hour later, everyone was in place. Dido, Tanya, Helen and Man stood around the wooden table in the command post. Staring at a map.

"What can you tell me about this William Nathan Bedford Forest?"

Nat had returned by this time.

"Everyone's in position suh," the young man acknowledged.

"So, what can you tell me?"

"Typical, plantation owner, slave owner, racist. Went from a private to a general in less than a year. They say that he's a great military strategist. Bottom line though is that he hates the Colored man," Dido commented.

"Then let's give him a good reason for his hate." Tanya chimed in lighting her pipe.

"And you're sure everyone is in place?" Dido asked.

"Yes suh," Nat answered anxious to see his first battle.

"Then man your positions and wait for my command." Dido said barking orders and feeling comfortable in his new role. It had only been a year since he'd commanded his own regiment and now back in his old role he knew that the survival of Maroon depended on he and he alone. Another rider came galloping in.

"Suh!" the young rider shouted jumping from his horse. "The confederate general requests a parley with you suh."

"Did he specify anyone specifically son?"

"No, suh. He just said he wanted to speak to the treasonous Cracker leading these niggas."

"Okay. Good. So that tells me that he neither knows who or what he's dealing with. A good military man usually has scouted and knows the size and strength of the unit he's about to go up against.

This General Nathan Bedford Forest knows nothing other than the fact that a rather large contingent departed from here and probably figures there's nothing left but a few stragglers that appear to be a pushover. And that's good. Let's allow him to think that. His own ego will end up being his undoing. He's known to be a great horseman and cavalry officer but in a battle such as this there is really no place to employ his cavalry. That is unless we allow him to…" Dido said smiling. "Send a messenger and tell him that there is no one to meet with. Tell him that there are only the old folks and infirmed that remain. Everyone else left to join the war."

"Yas, suh. But excuse me suh. I don't believe I know what infirmed means," the young man said.

Man was forced to smile.

"Tell him that there are only the sick and old left here," Dido replied patiently. "Tell him he is welcome to come in and see for himself."

And with that the plan was born. Once the Confederate cavalry was allowed to cross the bridge and enter Maroon the third and fourth regiments would ambush them with everything they had to muster while the newly formed first and second regiments would commence shelling the remainder of Bedford's troops.

It was hard to dispel General Nathan Bedford Forest's knowledge and acumen when it came to military strategy but if there was one intangible that both Dido and Man knew they could always count on was their adversaries' perception of the Niggra being inferior and it was this perception that had always given the army of Maroon a distinct advantage.

Today proved no different and in less than an hour Maroon scouts reported that about half of Forrest's cavalry of close to a thousand men were headed towards the bridge intent on entering Maroon.

"Hold fast and do not do anything until they have all crossed the bridge and are well within," Dido commanded. "This way we will have divided their forces then bombard them with all the heavy artillery we have. Helen, I want your sharpshooters to concentrate on Bedford's big guns and the general. Cut off the head and the body will follow. And may the good Lord bless all of you and keep you safe."

It was this undermining of the Coloreds that drove Bedford's cavalry across the drawbridge and a quarter of a mile inside the colony. Far off to the left of the road sat a few modest dwellings but there were no elderly or infirmed as reported and the captain who led the ruse turned in his saddle to order the cavalry back when Dido ordered the attack.

"Fire at will men!"

The bugle sounded and the air was filled with smoke as cannons and artillery filled the air. Helen and Tanya's troops took careful aim and the young captain who'd ordered his men to retreat was suddenly dislodged from his saddle. A bullet striking him in the temple. Caught in the heated crossfire Bedford's cavalry scrambled from their mounts desperately seeking cover but there was none to be found.

Those that remained on their mounts raced desperately back towards the bridge only to find that the drawbridge they'd only crossed minutes before no longer existed.

Instead a large contingent led by young Nat laid down a steady barrage of gunfire.

Bedford, surprised by this sudden turn of events ordered the artillery to fire.

"They're out of range sir," the young lieutenant responded.

"Then move in. Get closer. Do what you have to do lieutenant but dislodge those niggas. No quarter. No mercy. Do you hear me?" he screamed.

It was all to no avail as Helen's sharpshooters took careful aim and with pinpoint accuracy laid waste to the artillery men intent on moving closer.

"We're out of range and under heavy fire general!" the young lieutenant reported.

"Do what you have to do lieutenant. I want them niggas dislodged" Bedford shouted. And with that said the young lieutenant took what was left of his regiment had them regroup and proceeded to have them mount a charge but these men used to

286

fighting in a more traditional style were quite surprised when Roman Nose ordered his braves to attack.

Harassing them with charges from the perimeter and both flanks before moving out of range the young lieutenant ordered his men to stand pat. When they did attempt to lift their heads and advance it was Helen an Tanya's sharpshooters who picked them off like frantic, fowl in a turkey shoot.

"Sir, they have us pinned down."

"And what of the men who crossed the bridge?" Bedford cried desperately.

"There's been no word general and the bridge has been lifted. I fear they have been all but taken out. There is one survivor who swam back sir."

"Then bring him to me."

"Yes sir."

Moments later the young lieutenant returned with the lone cavalry survivor.

"What's the situation corporal?"

The corporal who appeared in shock could barely speak stood before the general in a trance-like state.

"Corporal! Report!" Bedford yelled. The corporal was visibly shaken.

"Neva seen so many niggas in my life suh. They hit us 'bout half a mile or more inside the front gates. Hit us with howitzers, cannons, Gatling guns and caught us in the crossfire. It was a pre-planned ambush, suh. I don't believe there was a man left standing, suh."

"Goddamn abolitionists. Had to be a white man behind this. Niggas ain't capable of this. Goddamn Yankees. Tell the men to stay low and sound the retreat."

"But general there may be survivors and we never leave a man behind, suh."

"We lost close to a regiment today son. I will not lose another man. I'm sorry to say that sometimes we have to yield to a higher power so that we may live to fight another day." Bedford said to everyone and no one in particular.

"But to a bunch of Niggas?"

"Believe me son. This ambush wasn't planned by no Niggas."

Two days later the Maroon army had what was left of William Bedford's army totally surrounded and at their mercy. It was only then that the white flag of truce was flown.

"We have forty-eight confirmed deaths and our hospital is full of our wounded, many of whom won't pull through, Man. And for what? We did nothing to incur this attack. I say we show no quarter and no mercy," Tanya shouted to all within earshot. She was immediately met with cheers from most of the soldiers many if not all who had lost friends and loved ones. And though both Dido and Man sympathized with their brothers neither had a wish to see anymore unnecessary bloodshed.

Man went out to meet Bedford under the white flag of truce.

"You men have come out of your way intent on doing us harm. We have shown no aggression on our part although you have done your best to maim and kill us. Still, and although most of my soldiers feel that you should be shown no quarter and no mercy my orders come from above. And He does not give me the right to take another man's life no matter the crime. It is a decree that I must follow and therefore I feel compelled to let you go free. This is something I doubt that you would've done had the choice been yours.

I will ask however that you leave everything aside from your pants and walk away with the quickness as I am apt to change my mind when I look and see my dead comrades and have to explain to their loved ones why they were killed for no other reason than your own blind hatred. Now if you would please drop all of your belongings and get before I have a change of heart!"

A week later Man received a message by way of telegraph from Dido who'd gone back to Washington to make sure the soldiers from Maroon were given equal pay as the white Union soldiers. The telegraph read of how a militia of some three hundred men had attacked the convoy carrying Major General William Forrest Bedford killed the envoy and freed the major who was once again reigning havoc against Union forces.

Thomas Man had never kept anything from Tanya but he knew telling her would only result in her saying 'I told you so' and so for once he hesitated in telling her this latest bit of news.

And for the first time since they'd been married she seemed content to occupy herself with the everyday efforts of simply running the community. She still came home physically exhausted but then who wouldn't after training the new recruits for the ladies auxiliary, and acting as sheriff of a growing and thriving Maroon. And being that Helen was pregnant again it lead to even more responsibility. Umi was in D.C. with Dido for their honeymoon so T was also in charge of the library. All in all it was a bit much but there was little or no inclination to want to fight any more on her part and of this Man was deeply relieved.

Helen did her best to make the rounds and check on her recruits who still served as perimeter scouts for the bonus pay. She made this a requirement to check on them each night before settling in as her girls were like her daughters.

Lately, T had accompanied her on these rounds and it was on just one of these nights that T, Helen and her oldest daughter Harriet got into the coach D had given her on their last anniversary and headed out. Both women were heavily armed, as slavers and bandits were out in droves since the war started and runaways were frequent and at a premium.

The driver of the coach Little Big Man had been assigned by Roman Nose as part of a security detail to watch over his friend Dante's family but on a quiet night such as this he was the lone one left to insure their well-being. On nights like these in which there was little to do Little Big man usually occupied his time talking to the now very lithe and very sexy Harriet on the front porch of her house. Helen rarely took the young man or anyone else with her when she made her rounds but with T and Harriet proposing to go she allowed the bored young man to drive her coach.

T and Helen sat comfortably inside while Harriet and her driver made small talk as they drove down one dusty road after another to check on the ladies hidden in small, hidden, encampments by the roadside.

It was a night like any other and the boy drove the carriage with a careful precision so as not to jar or cause the pregnant woman any discomfort.

"C"mon Little. I can walk faster than this. You can't be romancin' my daughter on my time. I have things to do and want to get back home. Now come on speed it up a tad," Helen said sticking her head out of the window of the coach. "Boy's so stuck on Harriet…"

"Ah, c'mon Helen. Leave them young folks alone. You remember when you were that age and Dante was courting you," T laughed. "Besides it's not often that we get out anymore just to relax and talk."

"You know Man is hating every minute you're not by his side." Helen teased.

"Gotta keep a little space between us or else I'll end up like you with a whole herd of young'uns followin' me around."

294

"I don't mind. In fact I love it. D said he wants ten and Lawd knows I love the practice. You don't know how much I miss my baby," Helen commented right before the carriage came to a lurching stop.

"What the hell? That boy," Helen yelled.

"Whatcha doin' boy," the skinny, tall, pock marked white man said grabbing the reins.

In all there were five men and a young boy about the same as Little Big Man. He couldn't have been more than seventeen or eighteen and it appeared all had been drinking more than their fair share.

"Whatcha carrying boy?"

"Davey check the carriage."

Davey a short, pudgy, white man rode up to the side of the carriage.

"Ain't nothin' but two nigga wenches," Davey replied.

"In a carriage as fine as this. These bitches done stole some rich, white man's carriage. Get them heifers out here so I can take a gander."

T instinctively went for her .45 revolver under her shawl when Helen put her hand on T's knee to stop her.

"There's five of them and only two of us and the kids are in the direct line of fire T. Let's play this out. They'll be another day for these bastards," Helen whispered in an attempt to calm her best friend down.

"I said git out of the goddamn carriage." The thin, tall, pock-faced man with the long, black hair and obviously the leader of the pack commanded. There was a short pause before the youngest of them, a sandy haired boy was ordered to get the women.

"This young one here is right nice just the way I likes mine. I likes them young and vibrant. You decide you wants to keep her you justs let me know son. Bout time you took a woman of your own and this one here will do you right nice 'til you find a white woman to call your own. Take her back out there in the woods and test her while we tend to these other two."

"I'm okay pa," the sandy haired boy replied.

"What the hell is wrong with you Luke? You know people are beginning to talk. Good lookin' boy like you not showin' any interest in women. Is you funny or somethin' boy? None of ya brothers woulda hadda problem wit' takin' a fine lookin' nigga inta woods and politickin' wit' her fine ass."

"I'm not my brothas poppa." The young man replied at which time his father backhanded him so hard the young man hit the ground.

"Now do as I say and take her in the woods and lay that pipe to her like a man and stop actin' like a goddamn sissy," the father said pushing Harriet in his direction. It was then that Little Big Man jumped down from the coach and yelled, "Noo!"

The red-faced father drew his revolver and fired twice. The first shot hit Little Big Man in the shoulder spinning him around to face the shooter at which time he shot again hitting the boy right above the heart. He was dead before he hit the ground.

"Now git!" the old man said to his son.

Seeing this Helen grabbed Tanya by the arm and squeezed hard, hoping to hold her back.

The son shocked by his father's actions pushed Harriet into the woods and no sooner had they become invisible he yelled.

"Run gal. Git the hell outta here."

"But that's my mama," Harriet screamed.

"Worry about yo'self gal and git the hell outta here before you wind up like your friend. Pa's drunk."

Harriet took off like the wind, ignoring the low-hanging branches that smacked against her face and arms. Heeding the young white boy's advice she continued running like someone was dead on her heels until she reached the gates of Maroon.

Meanwhile the older red-faced, white man known one passed the bottle of moonshine around to his colleagues as they eyed the two women now.

"Ain't neither one of 'em bad," the short, pudgy one added, "for niggas."

"Ain't bad?" the tall man, and leader of the entourage commented, "I don't know where you been hanging out Davey but these is two of the finest nigga wenches I seen in quite a spell. Either one of them could bring fifteen hundred to two grand down in Natchez. But before I even think about that we gonna test 'em out. I may even keep that young one. She looks strong and has some good child-bearing hips on her."

"Don'tcha think we might wanna get some information on these coons first John. They could be the personal concubines of some high falutin' planter down in New O'leans. Ain't nebba seen no niggas dressed dat well—betta than a lot of white womens— and just look at da carriage. We may git a lot mo' n reward money iffen we jes let 'em be."

"You could be right Davey but to me a niggas a nigga no matter how dey dressed and I's gonna have my way wit' both of these here gals befo' the night is over. You can best believe dat. But you could be right Davey. Bring 'em closer to me and in da light so I can see 'em mo' clearer.

"Say nigga," the leader of the pack said. "Where is you from and whose carriage is you driving?"

Helen realizing that T was enraged quickly answered not allowing T to speak. Any words from Tanya could only lead to their demise and things could not look any bleaker than they already appeared.

"Suh, massa 'llowed us to attend my sista's wedding here and gonna be mighty upset that you shot and killt his favorite driver suh. I's suggest you let us go on 'bout our way so we can get back home befo' our papers run out suh," Helen said in her best slave dialect.

"Is that right?" the long haired man replied taking another swig from the jug of moonshine. "And where are these papers?"

Helen let go of T's arm just enough to dig through her satchel and found papers that she'd written some time ago just for occasions such as this. Snatching the papers from her he attempted to read them and then passed them on to the one they called Davey.

"You know I cain't read. Tell me iffen what she sayed is true Davey."

"Everything seems to be just as she sayed it is John. Seems dey from Austin, Texas and is on route to a wedding here."

"Well, that's all well and good but dey is gonna be my treat tonight. Lost damn near every slave I got when Lincoln set 'em free. Mos' a dem ran when he come out wit' dat dere Emancipation Documentation. Lost over ten including two of my best heifers. We gonna see jes how dese stock up though. Davey, you and Pete strip these two naked and hogtie them to the wheels of this here carriage and don't lay a hand on 'em 'til I gits back. I'm gonna go check on dat dere sissy of a son of mine. Like ta have a taste of dat young meat first anyways," he grinned before taking another sip from the jug of moonshine.

Harriet hadn't stopped to catch her breath and upon entering the gates of Maroon and seeing the perimeter guard she passed out. Her brother Nat saw her racing towards him and rushed out he caught her as she was falling.

"Harriet!" he screamed. "What's wrong?"

Having difficulty catching her breath Nat took his canteen off and gave her some water.

"Mama!" she shouted.

"What about mama?" Nat asked his panic obvious now.

"They killed Little Big Man and have mama and Aunt T."

"Who has mama?"

"The slavers. Tell Uncle Thomas!" she said trying to put everything in proper perspective.

Nat not sure of what was transpiring sent two of his men to see man and report what Harriet had told him. Tempted to ride out he stayed with his sister who was now in and out of consciousness and suffering from shock.

Meanwhile, the slave catcher searched the forest for his son and the young slave girl. Cursing when he was unable to locate the two he made his way back to the road where the carriage stood. The two women were stripped naked and spread eagle, their legs overlapping when John the man in charge approached.

"Guess that boy a mine had otha plans for that wench. Both of 'em is gone," he chuckled as he dropped his suspenders to his sides and unzipped his coveralls. "Don't know which of dese here bitches I want first," he laughed. "Betta start wit' dat dere young one," he said referring to T. "She looks like she gonna require a lil' mo' work so I may as well start wit' her," he joked lifting the jug as he kicked her legs apart.

"Be strong T. We can get through this. Just you be strong," Helen said attempting to touch T's hand with her own.

"Shut up bitch!" the slaver said slapping Helen hard and busting her lip.

"Be strong T," Helen repeated despite the slaver backhanding her again knocking her out.

And then with all the force he could muster the tall, long haired gentleman was not so gentle entering T with all the force he could muster. His was a violent rage of twisted anger. Over and over he entered her until he had little left before doing the same to Helen. An hour later the other men were still going at the two women who'd passed out by now.

The sound of a rider could be heard approaching but the two men who were now taking liberties with Helen and Tanya did not stop their assault. It was the sheriff of Topeka.

"Hey sheriff," John said greeting the sheriff as if they'd all just come from a Sunday picnic at the local church.

"John," the sheriff replied. "Whatcha boys up to?"

"Not a lot. Just come across these here two runaways and me and da boys here is lettin' loose a lil' energy befo' returnin' dem to dere rightful owner and collectin' da reward."

The sheriff rode around the wagon in attempts to get a closer look.

"I'm afraid you may have bitten off a whole lot more than you can chew this time John," he said lifting T's head. "Dis here nigga is in charge of a group of free niggas. She's first or second in command. Got more than a thousand armed niggas behind her. I'm tellin' you John you done bit off mo' n' you can stand right through here. Dey rode into Topeka a few months ago dressed in all black and when we couldn't handle 'em I sent for the feds and dey whooped the feds asses too. What I suggest you do is make peace wit' these two da best way you can or dere's gonna be hell to pay."

"Dat don't even sound like you sheriff. I ain't nebba known you to cow tow to no niggas. Why don'tcha git down and have ya'self a taste. Dat dere young one's a feisty thang but I believe I done broke dat bronc. She's ready for a good ride right about now."

"I think I'll pass and I suggest you do the same. Iffen I was you I'd git as far away from here as I can. I'm tellin' you dere's gonna be hell to hell to pay when dese here women gits loose."

"And who's to say dey ever is gonna get loose?" John smirked tilting the half empty jug back up.

"I'm tellin' ya John. If ya gots any type of desire to live you's betta git back on ya horses and ride outta here wit' da quickness."

"C'mon John. Da sheriff knows betta than we do and iffen he says dese women is part of a nigga army den we best be gittin outta here befo' dey come lookin' for 'em. Besides we all

307

tuckered out from dem wenches anyway. Ain't nuthin' else ta be had from 'em."

"Okay. Okay. Damn, if y'all ain't a sorry lot. Gotta wait for Luke ta get back."

"You ain't hearin' da sheriff is you? Or has dat corn whiskey clouded yo' thinkin' John. You could look at dese niggas and see dat dey wasn't no run a da mill niggas. We done had our pleasure wit' 'em now let's get out while da getting' is good."

"Well, what about Luke? I jes cain't leave my boy here."

"Luke's probably home and in bed. Listen you can stay here if you like but me and da boys is leavin'."

"Ah, hell, let's ride."

Moments later Man rode in with a little over a hundred men. Nat was the first one in and seeing his mother and aunt he broke down. Blood and semen dripped down the inner thighs of both women. And though both were semiconscious Tanya did not utter a word. Helen, on the other hand, was cognizant of those around her and her surroundings.

"I'm okay Man. Have the women take T down to the river and clean her up. You stay with her until she comes to. Just hold her and tell her you love her. She's had a pretty rough go of it."

"And you?"

"I'll be fine. It's not the first time but let me grab Nat and some of the girl's and see if we can't catch up with those responsible for this. The sheriff of Topeka knows the men responsible for this but I doubt if he'll be of any help."

"Oh, he most definitely will be. Just wait until I get my hands on that son-of-a-bitch."

"No Man. Just take care of T for now. We can all go after him once she's back on her feet. Oh, and Man you might tell those with you to keep this news to themselves. I don't think T would want anyone to know."

"I gotcha," Man said dejectedly as he gazed at his wife who appeared despondent despite the three or four women bathing her and attempting to clean her up.

"How's she doing," Man asked Chastity Pettiway who led the cleanup crew.

"Don't know. Physically she' strong as an ox and in a few days maybe a week she'll be fine but that's not what bothers me. Her mind is not there right now. She's been traumatized and is still in a state of shock. There's no telling how long it'll take her for her to recover. All we can do is show her love and stay by her side in case she needs anything or wants to talk. That's about all we can do."

"Will you stay with her Chastity?"

"Helen and I have already decided to stay with her until we feel she's back on her feet. But like I said the best case scenario is that she'll bounce right back and if I know Miss T she'll want blood. The worst case scenario is that this may take months or even years. All we can do is pray about it."

"Thanks Chastity."

"No need to thank me. You and T have always been there for me. I'm only glad I can do something on your behalf."

Harriet was there helping to aid her mother. Helen was strong though and admonished her oldest daughter.

"What are you crying for? Little Big Man has gone on to a better place and your aunt and I are here to tell about it. We will have our revenge and you know as well as I do that those men who did this are the ones who you should feel for. The wrath of Allah is now upon them. They will attempt to run and hide and will spend the rest of their days looking over their shoulders until we

311

catch up with hem and then they will suffer as they never have before. So, there's no need to cry for us."

Nat had taken some thirty or forty troops and ridden off in the direction of the men but as it was already late it was difficult to pick up their trail. He promised to get up and continue his search but with the dawn came the rains washing all the tracks out.

Still, in the upcoming week Nat took a contingent out every day in search of the men who had taken liberties with his mother and aunt. Over and over, he asked Harriet to go over every detail of that night to the best of her recollection including every detail of the men until he had all but memorized their descriptions. And then at the end of his shift he would pick up and lead his men out traversing every farm and back road within a hundred miles of the crime scene. When convinced that he hadn't left a stone unturned he'd go back and start all over again.

T hadn't spoken at all since the attack. Papa called it a nervous breakdown but Man didn't see it that way and just considered his wife as being temporarily out of commission.

"If there's one thing I know about T is that she's a fighter and not a quitter. She will get over this or around this but if there's one thing I know about my wife it's that she will transgress the evil that's come her way and only become stronger with time. When she does recover I only feel sorry for those that chose to do this," Man would say.

But after three months without her uttering a word to anyone Thomas was having his doubts as well.

"Give her time Man," Helen said. "But trust me when she does come out of it the world will know it," Helen said smiling before placing a warm kiss on Man's cheek. During that time, T was tantamount to a vegetable frequently urinating and defecating on herself and was seemingly content to lie in wait of someone to come in and clean her up. She made no attempt to correct this or any other of her other problems and would stare blankly off into space for hours at a time responding to nothing and no one.

Both Helen and Chastity took their time and worked painstakingly to arouse anything in the young woman they had all come to refer to as T but it all seemed to no avail. And yet neither gave up hope.

The word quickly circulated around Maroon that the woman so many had come to address as 'The Queen' was suddenly relegated to being a has been. Her reign was short-lived and although her reign had been strong she was now all but passé. Young women now approached Man with all intents of becoming the new heir to the throne. Yet, despite everything Man remained steadfast in his undying love and devotion for his queen despite her apparent gloom and hopelessness.

Chapter 24

And then one morning at dawn T got up, dressed quickly and uttered the first words she'd said in months.

"Grab enough grub and provisions for two to three days Man. Summon the girls and have Helen, Nat and Harriet join us and be hasty. It's time to ride."

Man was too shocked to respond but proceeded fulfilling T's wishes as asked. It felt so good having her back in the fold he didn't know what to do.

An hour later, the party stood at the front gates to Maroon. Everyone there was in a jovial mood so happy were they to have the matriarch of Maroon back. And then the party started out at an easy gallop towards Topeka.

There was little in the way of conversation with T seemingly on a mission. Her undertaking unknown to anyone but her they followed her nonetheless and without question.

Once they'd reached Topeka T stopped at one of the local Colored tavern and boarding house where she and Helen went in and after ordering a couple of beers and after asking a number of questions they exited. Man was at a complete loss but was thankful that Helen was there.

In control now it was almost as if the woman he called his wife had not been gone at all. The only thing missing was the easy smile she was known for. No, this new T was stern and steadfast in whatever undertaking she was now on. Whatever the operation it was serious and for her there wasn't a moment to waste. To her way of thinking, she'd wasted too much time already.

"T we've ridden for close to twenty four hours straight. The girls and the horses are plumb tuckered out. Both need to rest or else neither will be any good once we get to the objective."

"Just a little while more then we'll rest for the night. I promise you Man," she said before kissing him long and hard. She grabbed his hand. "I just want to thank you for taking care of me these last few months. Thank you for continuing to love me despite all that's happened. And I want you to know that I'm aware of all those little fresh heifers that tried to pull you away from me when I was down. But you remained true and strong in your devotion and I'm grateful for that."

"C'mon T. What did you think? The least little adversity and I'm gonna tuck tail and run? That's what a good marriage is made out of. Adversity only seals the bond and makes one grow stronger. I married you for better or worse. It can't get any better and your worse is not even a little bothersome and do you know why?"

"No, why?" she smiled. It was the first smile she'd elicited in months and warmed Man's heart.

"Because I love me some T."

They hugged and then mounted their horses.

"No more than another hour or two," T announced.

The party oblivious to their eventual destination were more curious than tired and followed T in close pursuit. An half an hour later the party of close to twenty-five pulled up on a bluff overlooking a small farm down in the valley below.

The farm wasn't much and hardly resembled any of those on Maroon. Two or three cows grazed leisurely in the pasture below along with a horse or two grazing in the same pasture. An old rickety, buckboard leaned to its side and the cabin itself was not built well and had large gaps between the logs. It was obvious that whoever had designed it had little knowledge of architecture or carpentry as there were more flaws than one could shake a stick at.

Man had no idea who lived here but one thing he did know. This wasn't the home of the men who'd raped Tanya and Helen. He'd sent several teams out to seek information on who those men were and from all that he'd gathered back those men had vanished into thin air. Nat had also conducted his own investigation following every lead known to him and he had come up empty as well.

"Set up camp here!" T instructed and whatever you do keep the noise down to a minimum. This is no different than a scouting expedition ladies so you know better than to make a campfire after dark. And please do not smoke. The least amount of flicker or flame can give away our position. I know it's early but we've been riding almost all night so you should be exhausted. Lay down and get some rest. In the morning a man will come riding in. Helen and I will ride in. We have some business to conduct with this man. What I will need for you to do is to shut down the perimeter while we are inside parlaying with this white man. Make sure no one rides in or out. Shouldn't take us more than an hour at best. I will fully inform you of the proceedings when I return. Does anyone have any questions?"

Man had plenty but as he wasn't included in the briefing he refrained from asking anything. He had to learn to put his trust in her.

When he awoke the next morning the lone rooster on the farm below was crowing. Reaching out to feel his wife man felt nothing but the barren sleeping bag she'd gone to sleep in. Looking around he also noticed Helen's empty bag. Somewhat worried now he awoke the camp and instructed them to secure the perimeter while he rolled out of his bag grabbed his rifle, canteen, and his horse and made his way down carefully towards the tiny cabin below. Seeing Helen and T's horses Man dismounted his horse and found his way down to the corral. Sneaking around til' he made his way right outside the cabin window he knelt and then lifting his head he peeked in.

What he saw terrified even him. A very stately and handsome woman not more than forty or forty five years of age sat there tied to one of the wooden kitchen chairs completely naked.

"Perhaps you don't give a damn about your life or ours but perhaps you do give a damn about your wife's life," Helen stated matter-of-factly.

The sheriff of Topeka, the very same man who stood there when those men were raping Helen and T now sat tied to the chair in his very own cabin.

"You warned them that we'd be back to exact vengeance on them but you did little to protect us from any harm and as far as I know we are now your constituents and are entitled to protection under the law. I believe Mr. Lincoln made that clear and yet you let those men rape us."

"No you didn't Wyatt? You didn't stand idly by and let these po' women get raped."

"Shut up Mary. I'm not and have never been responsible for protecting the lives of niggas."

"But Wyatt these aren't niggas. These are people with feelings just like you and I have."

"I'm sorry to inform you ma'am but your husband doesn't necessarily see it that way. I suppose you'd be better inclined to watch the company you keep. He not only watched us be raped but forewarned his buddies about our coming back and seeking retribution. What he did was scare them off before they could be held accountable."

"Tell me this isn't true Wyatt," the comely redhead said seemingly shocked.

The embarrassed sheriff dropped his head.

"Yes, he did and I'm okay with that but I want those men's names before I gut you like the pig you are," Tanya said pulling out her Bowie knife and swiping it cutting off part of the sheriff's ear. Screaming in pain it wasn't clear what was to follow and the sheriff cried out.

"Johnathan Johnson. His name is Johnathan Johnson," The sheriff shrieked holding up his hands to prevent himself from any further harm but it was Helen who took the initiative this time and nailed his hand to the kitchen table with her own butcher knife.

"And where can we find this Johnathan Johnson?" Helen asked.

323

"Down by Willow Creek at the fork in the road. He has a small farm but he hasn't been seen since the attack on you two," the sheriff confided hoping that the two would do no more damage.

"I do believe that's all we came for? Gut the bastard Helen." At which time Helen shoved the Bowie knife into the sheriff's stomach just below the navel and dragged it up until it reached the man's throat.

His wife's screams were loud enough to wake the neighbor's on the adjoining farms but T made quick work of her as well slitting her throat on the way out the door.

"Gotta be cognizant of the company you keep," T remarked closing the door and leaving the two corpses slumped over on the floor inside.

Man still kneeling and too stunned to move remained looking in the window when the women came out and spoke.

"Good morning Thomas," Helen said as if nothing had happened.

Thomas still unable to speak stood there.

"I'm sorry you had to witness that sweetheart. That's why Helen and I broke camp before anyone got up. We were just gathering a little intelligence is all," T said smiling. "But come on. We still have one other little mission to accomplish."

Still dumbfounded Thomas mounted his horse while Tanya and Helen circled the tiny cabin pouring kerosene around the foundation. Moments later Tanya tossed a box of matches, then watched the house go up in flames and yelled.

"Let's ride."

They rode back to the camp in silence gathered the rest of the party and started out on the second leg of their journey. All but Man, Helen and T knew their destination as smoke from the burning cabin billowed high in the background.

325

Five miles later they pulled up outside of a small farm on the other side of Topeka. Fields of cotton met them and several hands could be seen working in the distance. Riding up to the woman closest to her Tanya dismounted.

"Excuse me ma'am but could you tell me where I could locate a Mr. John Johnson?"

"Lawd gal iffen you don't look and talk like white folk," the woman said staring at T before turning her gaze to the rest of the party. "Say, where is you niggas from. I know y'all ain't from 'round here. Y'all is high falutin'. Don't see no niggas dressed like y'all wit' yo fine horses. Lucious," she yelled at a Colored man two rows over. "Come take a look at dese niggas. You ain't nebba seen no niggas like dese."

The old Colored man wandered over. He did not seem the least bit flustered as had the woman.

"How y'all doin'?" he asked trying his best to be cordial though it was obvious he was beaten down and on his last leg.

"I'm good suh. I was just wondering if you knew of a Mr. John Johnson. They say he has a farm around these parts."

"Lawd you ain't even say nothin' bout the way dese here niggas talk. Almost like white folk dey do. You cain't tell me you useta seein' niggas like dis Lucius," the woman commented.

"Plenty of upstandin', well-spoken Coloreds in Boston and New O'leans," Lucius commented.

"Ah, stop yo' lyin nigga. You ain't nebba been ta no Boston or New O'leans."

Ignoring the loud mouthed old woman Lucious went on.

"This is Masta Johnson's place ma'am." He said grabbing the reins of T's horse and rubbing the horse's nose. "Fine lookin' horse ya got here ma'am."

"Thank you suh. You said this is John Johnson's place. Could you tell me where I could find him right about now?"

"Sure. Take this rode straight up about a quarter mile or so and you should see his house on the right hand side. There's a mulberry bush in the front yard or better yet what's left of it. He should be sitting there on the front porch if I know him."

"Thank you kindly suh and by the way do you know of a man named Davey. He's a short, pudgy, red-faced white man as well as…"

Tanya went on to describe the rest of the party that had gone about accosting she and Helen some months before and the elderly gent they called Lucius went on to give the whereabouts of them all.

"I'm taking this ain't no cordial visit Miss…?"

Lucius remarked.

"No names needed at this time but you can come see the show if you care to. Lucius is it?"

"Yes ma'am, I surely would but if I leave these fields Masta Johnson wouldn't have no qualms about laying the whip to me and I ain't young as I used ta be. Might kill me now bad as I would like to see the show."

"Trust me Lucius. John Johnson will never lay a hand on you again. That I promise you."

"Don't be stupid Lucius. You don't know these niggas from Adam's house cat but you do know what Massa will do to you if he hears of you fraternizin' wit' dese here niggas. You may be a tad bit older but I been around long enough to knows trouble when I sees it and dese here niggas ain't nothin' but trouble."

"C'mon miss I'll show you where he is," Lucius said grabbing the horse and leading it up the road.

"You so stupid Lucius. I don't know how you made it dis far. Dey say God takes care of babies and fools. And you sho is a fool. Just rememba' ain't no one gonna take care of yo ass when massa gets a whim of you and dese here niggas. Dey trouble. I'm tellin' you Lucius. Dey is shonuff trouble," the woman yelled as the party made its way up the road.

A quarter of a mile up the road they found John Johnson just as Lucius said he would be sipping from a jug just the same as he had been when he'd run across Tanya and Helen that night.

"Whatcha y'all want?" Massa John shouted to the group pulling up and stopping before the porch.

"We're here to see a Mr. John Johnson," Man said to the white man sitting.

"I'm John Johnson and I don't 'llow no niggas but da one's dat works fo' me on my place," he said to the group before him.

"Things done changed Mr. Johnson. We niggras is here to hold you accountable for crimes you committed against some of our kinfolk."

"Nigga iffen you don't get the hell offa m'land I'll have every last one of you whipped. You hear me?"

Before he could continue Man had gotten down off his horse and made his way onto the porch. Nat was by his side and was intent on taking the man's head off when Man grabbed him.

"Let your mother decide his fate Nat. After all it was she who had to suffer under this man's hand. Show some restraint son."

"Listen nigga. Maybe you didn't hear me. If you don't git da hell off of my land I'll have all of y'all whipped."

"Didn't I tell you dese niggas won't nothin' but trouble Lucius," the old woman who'd been in the fields said poking Lucius.

By this time T and Helen stood before John Johnson.

"Remember us?" Helen asked her eyes gleaming with a fiery hatred.

Before he could answer Tanya took out the Colt .45 she carried on her hip and let off a shot hitting the lanky, white man in the upper thigh. John Johnson let a curdling scream and reached out to grab the woman that shot him. Moving deftly from his grasp she then ordered Nat.

"Round up the rest of these Crackers and bring them to me."

An hour later, Nat and the girls were back at the Johnson farm with the five other men who'd been privy to the attack on Helen and Tanya. Man then took control of the proceedings as the men were lined up on the porch of the cabin.

"These five men are accused of raping these two women and have now been identified and are hereby sentenced to death.

332

Usually an offense such as this is punishable by death but in this particular case and because of the horrendous nature of this crime which includes rape and sodomy we will allow the women who fell victim to decide these men's fate," Man decreed stepping off the porch allowing Harriet, Helen and T to come forward to decide the men's fate. Harriet came forth fist.

"There is no doubt in my mind that these men in question committed a horrible crime and I seek no mercy or compassion when it comes to them. And I fear I would have suffered the same fate as my mother and my auntie if it hadn't been for Mr. Johnson's son Luke. I therefore ask that his sentence be commuted," Harriet said. "That is only justice."

"And do you think that would've been done if the tables had been turned?" Tanya asked.

"No, I don't auntie but I think we are better than that. I don't think any one of us at Maroon would have even considered committing such crimes. We niggras just ain't built that way," she commented to all present.

Man couldn't have been more proud and jumped in before T or Helen had a chance to speak.

"And it is therefore decreed that Luke the son of John Johnson's son has been commuted. He will be imprisoned and stand trial at a later date for being in the company of these men but will not stand trial for the rape and sodomy of these women. It will also be noted at his trial date that he assisted in the escape of one Harriet Black. Ladies, you may proceed with the trial of the aforementioned defendants."

Lucius stood there smiling with pride. When Man was finished he approached him slowly whispering to him.

"Once again it has been brought to my attention that additional charges have been levied against Mr. John Johnson by his own hands and former slaves."

"Nigga I'll have you whipped 'til you're bloody when this farce is over," John Johnson proclaimed as he did everything to stop his leg from bleeding from the bullet wound.

Ignoring his remarks Man stepped back onto the porch.

"It has been brought to my attention by Lucius that over the years Mr. Johnson has exacted cruel and unusual punishment over his charges resulting in the hanging deaths of a half a dozen of his own slaves including Lucius' wife Claudine who refused to let her bed her down.

Mr. Lucius' own son Frederick was given fifty lashes and had his eye put out for not picking in excess of a hundred pounds of tobacco in a day. He was given fifty lashes, his eye was put out and his mother killed because of John Johnson's cruelty and barbarism. We will allow him to seek retribution now but not in access of fifty lashes. Will that do you justice Lucius?"

The old man nodded in agreement and his son stood up and picked up the whip. T's girls grabbed John Johnson and dragged the screaming man to the old sycamore tree where he was tied and stripped to the waste. Given the whip Frederick looked to his father.

"Father you've suffered more than I have at the hands of this man. Your wife and my mother was killed for upholding her marriage vows and choosing not to sleep with Massa John. So, if you want to whip him feel free. I believe you have suffered much more than I have at this man's hands. I've only lost an eye. You've lost the love of your life. Let the honor be yours."

"Beat the hell out of him my son. He is not worth me lifting my hand to. He is beneath me."

With that said Frederick picked up the whip and laid the whip to the man's back as if there were no tomorrow but stopped just short of twenty times.

"These ladies have been transgressed far worse than I have and are due retribution and if I continue I fear I will kill him. Besides I cannot inflict the harm that he has imposed on me and mine," Frederick said eloquently enough before moving aside.

The woman who'd worked beside Lucius in the field came close to fainting when she saw Frederick lay the whip to her massa.

"Oh Lawdy Jesus help me and pray for my soul. Da world done been turnt upside down," she screamed. "You gots niggas beatin' white folks. Lawd knows y'all going to hell fo' sho. You done sold your very soul ta da devil Lucius. Lawd help him Jesus." she screamed before falling out.

"Give her some water," Man ordered. "Tanya, Helen let's do this and get it over with. Time's a wastin' and we need to get out of here," Man said to the two women now in charge. "Let justice be done."

No sooner than he said that than T whipped out the same Bowie knife she'd used on the sheriff and approached John Johnson who screamed every vile epitaph he had in his arsenal.

"You Black heathen. Y'all is writing yo' own epitaph. Y'all betta not lay a hand on me you nigga bitch. Y'all niggas is violating the very same bible you is quotin' from. I know y'all know Paul: 'Servants, be obedient to them that are your masters according to the flesh, with fear and trembling," he said quoting scripture.

"Y'all betta take heed or suffer the wrath of God," Massa John Johnson said pleading the only case he knew only to have it fall on deaf ears as Diola and Tiffany pulled his pants down to his knees.

Man, unable to stomach what T were to do next took Nat, Harriet and Luke and whoever else chose to leave and had them run security from John Johnson's farm to his neighbor's all of whom had been pronounced guilty and awaited prosecution.

"Leave his pants down around the ankles so he doesn't flail all around. I want him to be confined when I slice his dick into ribbons," Helen said calmly and with much resolve. And then taking T's Bowie knife she sliced a small incision in his left scrotum that brought tears to his eyes and made him call out to a Jesus he had yet come to know.

Taking her time she went down he row of men doing the same to each of them. Once she finished she went back to the beginning and sliced tiny slits in each of the men's penises. When she was finished she asked each of the men if they remembered her.

"Was it worth it? In your Bible and I am not a big fan of it although I have read it it plainly states in Luke.

'And will not God give justice to his elect, who cry to him day and night? Will he delay long over them? I tell you, he will give justice to them speedily'.

Now in your case, I am doing His work and will do you your justice speedily. My sister, on the other hand, may interpret your Bible much differently but I am finished seeking justice. I now leave your fate up to her," Helen said to each of the men now writhing and groaning in pain.

By the time T made her way to the men the front porch was a pool of blood. Taking the Bowie from Helen Tanya went up to each man pushed their heads back and slit each of their throats.

"Bury them and let's ride! Better yet drag their corpses inside and torch the house."

Tanya was already on her horse when the house was set ablaze. Then she addressed those that remained.

"We have a small community of free, independent, Black folks. We call it Maroon and it's been in existence for close to thirty years. All of you who worked for these men no longer have to. You are free and can own your own land and join our community should you choose to. But our time is limited. Should you choose to grab your belongings hitch up a couple of plow horses to one of his wagons? We'll be pulling out in less than half an hour so be prepared and ready to go. We don't have time to waste. I'm sure someone will be here as soon as they see the smoke."

Lucius summoned his son Frederick and made plans to join the party along with the fifteen or twenty other slaves on the plantation. The older woman who objected vehemently and passed out when she saw her master whipped was revived and now reasserted her beliefs.

"All y'all niggas is crazy. Y'all ungrateful like massa always said. Ya done broke da commandments and now y'all gonna jes gonna steal his horse and cart and ride off wit' some ol' crazy high-falutin niggas ya ain't nebba seen befo'. And afta all massa done done for y'all," she screamed as the wagon was ready to pull off.

"We gonna see how much they appreciate you when they come to find all of them missin' white folks and only you here to explain," Lucius explained.

It didn't take her long to comprehend and soon she was running to catch the wagon as it pulled off.

Chapter 25

The weather had turned nippy upon their return due to the frigid northeasterly winds blowing in off the mountain and Man was thankful for this. Most of Maroon's townsfolk were secure in their homes and bungalows and for this Man was grateful

There were no questions concerning the prior days or this morning's activities. He didn't want to think about it although he had countless times on the ride back. Few words had been spoken on the ride back and T. seemed oblivious to the silence.

It bothered Man to no end though. This woman he thought so warm and careful had eliminated—no murdered—seven people without a second thought and this had nothing to do with what papa chose to refer to as a nervous breakdown. No. From what he understood this and occurrences like this had happened prior this. There was the time the women under her command sat around the campfire and spoke of how she'd slit their captives throats as if it were nothing. To her it was no different than slicing a cantaloupe or watermelon.

It had affected him then but to see it up close and personal was something he knew he would never forget. He was sure now that something or someone had done something so devastating, so traumatizing that she would never forget and mama's influence on her had done nothing but to make her anger and hatred grow worse. The rape and everyone involved in it seem to only intensify it. He seriously wondered if she'd ever open up and talk about it but in his heart he knew that it was over until or at least the next opportunity presented itself.

Wasn't this the same person who had opted for a church being built? He wondered how she could incorporate the teachings of Jesus into this kind of behavior. Hadn't Jesus been the one who prophesized and spoken of turning the other cheek and said vengeance was his? Hadn't she heard? Hadn't she even considered papa's teaching when it came time and he had the opportunity to wreak vengeance on a beaten foe? He never had. He never would. And yet it was almost as if she'd turned a deaf ear to all his teachings. He wondered if she would even bring it up and talk to him about it. These he knew despite the transgressions bestowed on her that revenge was the utmost thought in her mind. All he could do was hope that she too would have a day of thought, of reckoning that there was more to revenge than the act of vengeance and that there was a day when she too would have to own up to her own actions instead of letting the hate inside her consume her. But still she did not speak of the hatred of the events that had forced her to kill both the sheriff and his wife.

Arriving home he found all as it was when he left. The servants, to whom they paid a tidy sum had everything as it was when they left. A pot of homemade oxtail soup lay on the still warm, kindling smoldering on top of the wood burning stove.

Dipping a healthy portion for he and T, Man sat down at the dining room table and poured them both a glass full of the blackberry wine papa had grown so good at making.

"So, Ms. T. Tell me how you feel after exacting revenge on those that violated you?" he asked.

It took a while for T. to answer and he knew that the question had evoked considerable thought.

"You know Man, I listened to papa and hear mama. I guess I am not quite as strong in some respects as you and papa. And I know that both of you are probably right in your reactions to those who commit these transgressions but I guess I interpret the bible and its teachings differently than you do but I cannot get past the part of 'an eye for an eye'. I suppose you think I'm a bit touched but I cannot let these men continually transgress not only me but everyone that resembles me simply because they can.

Something in me just won't allow that to continually happen. And from what I understand of this war that pits brother against brother there are quite a few others that feel the same way that I do. Might does not make right and too many Colored soldiers have flocked to the Union side and are willing to fight to let that be known. Too many of us believe that because they hold the upper hand that they are right in oppressing us but there are a right many of us that don't believe that just because they have superior firepower that they are entitled to make us no more than chattel, no more than cows or farm animals to be used at their discretion so they can gain great wealth at our expense. Nat Turner, David Walker and people like Harriet Tubman let them know that. But what is even more important is the fact that in every little town and hamlet we are fighting this injustice. We burn and poison and resist in every possible way because and even though we are not or haven't been successful in overturning this peculiar institution called slavery we are committed to do just that and I want to be as active in helping to overthrowing this charade as any of my people. And I don't give a second thought to maiming or killing any man or woman who tries to impose his authority on me including that racist sheriff or his wife."

"I hear you and understand you T. but in reality his wife had nothing to do with him and his actions."

"If you were to steal one of Masters hogs and I was with you would I not be considered an accomplice? What is it they say? 'Birds of a feather flock together'. Like I told her be careful of the choices you make and the company you keep. By now, and this late in their marriage she had to know this man had no regard for a niggra. She even admitted so when she asked him 'what has he done now'. And being that he was filled with so much hate and contempt towards us Coloreds he refused to show any pain when harm came to him. Don't you see it was the only way I could open his eyes. I knew he had to have a soft spot and she was it. He was so calloused he couldn't feel any pain but he felt hers. That's why she had to suffer. I'm sorry I am not at your level as of yet my husband but believe me I am working to become a better person." She said dropping her head. Man knew she was sorry if for nothing else than he having to witness her own hatred.

"This is one of the reasons I got up early and rode on ahead. I didn't want you to see what I felt necessary to do," she said walking behind him and wrapping her hands around his shoulders. I apologize. I am so sorry you had to witness that my husband."

"There's no need to apologize T. I am so glad to finally have you back in the fold that there's hardly anything you could do that would warrant an apology."

"You're beautiful, Man."

The two toasted each other over another glass of wine before she grabbed his hand and led him to the bedroom where they spent most of the night making passionate love.

The following morning, they were awakened by a rider who thundered in at a gallop. This was never a good sign and the news he brought couldn't have been worse.

"Man, suh."

"Yes, corporal." Man said pulling up the bib of his coveralls and taking out his corncob pipe as he always did in the anticipation of bad news.

"Suh, there's news from the front, suh," the young man stated.

"Hold on son," Man said waiting for his second to arrive. When T. was by his side and he'd had the occasion to take a long pull off his pipe he prompted the young soldier to continue.

"Corporal."

"Suh, it seems that some three hundred Colored soldiers were massacred at Fort Pillow, Tennessee. Most if not all were from Maroon. Yas suh, three of the six hundred men guarding Fort Pillow were Colored soldiers from right here in Maroon. Seems that Major General Nathan Bedford Forest, the very same one that we allowed his freedom had some twenty-five hundred men and surrounded the fort. When the Colored soldiers realized their cause was futile they threw up the white flag of surrender. Seems he ignored it for no other reason that the fact that they were Colored and cut them down in cold blood. Says he didn't recognize them as soldiers but as nigga contraband. Seems that your friend Dante was shot first being that he was their commander."

"Thank you corporal," Man said dropping his head and letting the tears flow freely.

Tanya feeling her husband's pain, grabbed Man by those broad shouldered that seemed so frail right now and led him back into the house. No sooner than they entered the door Man fell to the Queen Elizabeth chair and howled.

"Lord God why are they so intent on doing what they do? We didn't ask to be brought here. Neither did we asked to be enslaved and now that we have been emancipated they see no other choice than to exterminate us. Why oh why Lord, do they choose to persecute us so? We showed compassion and allowed Nathan Bedford to escape when we could have very well wiped him and his whole party out but we showed compassion and this is how he repays us. Slaughtering three hundred Colored troops for no other reason than the color of their skin? Why lord? Please tell me why?"

"And you ask me I am so filled with anger and bitterness?" Tanya said with little sympathy other than for her husband who now wept openly his shoulders shuddering deeply with each thought that now arose over the atrocities committed.

"If I were you my love I would take an army of equal or more soldiers and strike back with the same horror and indignity that he has shown. I would make him pay dearly with his life and the lives of his men. That's what I would do."

The sobering thought of T's words crossed Man's mind and retaliation certainly seemed a suitable recourse and then just as quickly as it entered his mind he thought of papa and what papa would have done had he been posed with the same situation.

Yes, his lifelong friend had been executed in a way that was in no way fit or appropriate under the protocol of warfare but no there was no need for retaliation. If he was truly a believer in Christ the Lord he was certain that the devil would have his due. But it was not for him to seek retribution. It was his right to grieve for his friend and pick up the pieces where Dante had left off in rearing his passel of children, now abandoned in this hideous war but that was as far as his duties would allow him to go. And there was no better time to do this than the present. But first he would call a gathering and spread the word of this terrible tragedy and then go and speak to the families of then men slaughtered in this terrible massacre. That's what he would do before asking for volunteers to replace those men. Deep down inside he wondered if this wasn't God's way of sending a message to him for condoning Tanya's actions of the prior day. He had to wonder. But for now he had to go see Helen personally and share the news.

Knocking on the door of Helen's palatial home he felt his hands trembling and wondered if he would make it through this momentous hurdle.

"Hey Man," she said giving him a brotherly hug as he entered. "And what may I ask brings you here on such a cold, brisk day?"

Hardly able to look the, big, buxom woman in the eye Helen sensed something was amiss.

"Sit, Man and tell me what's on your mind."

Man dropped his head and Helen knew whatever it was it wasn't good.

"I'm afraid I have some bad news from the front."

"Concerning Dante?"

"I'm afraid so. Seems Major General Nathan Bedford Forrest led an assault on Fort Pillow where Dante and three hundred of our men were guarding the fort. Forrest had more than twelve hundred men and so Dante seeing that they were totally outnumbered and outgunned chose to surrender under a white flag of truce."

"Are we speaking of the same Nathan Bedford Forrest who tried to lay siege to Maroon some months back?"

"The very same."

"So, go ahead, Continue."

"In any case and because they were Colored soldiers he shot them down in cold blood. Yes, he shot them down under a white flag of truce. Three hundred men from Maroon with Dante stepping forward in front of his men holding the white flag was massacred, shot down in cold blood," Man said weeping openly now. "I am so terribly sorry Helen."

"Don't be," Helen said. "He was as much as your friend as he was mine and if I know my man if he had to go he would have wanted to go in such a manner. As we both know he was as much a warrior and a fighter as he was a father and husband. Dante died loving what he did so there are no need for tears, my brother. The children will take it hard but they'll adjust," she commented almost as if she'd somehow been waiting for this day to finally arrive.

"Now straighten up Man. We have to present a strong front for the children and the people as a whole."

If Man had ever had any question of who was the stronger sex it was put to rest now and he did his best to quarter his emotions.

Standing to his full height he bent over slightly to hug Helen and then eased toward the doorway.

"Do me a favor Man."

"Anything Helen."

"Be the one to tell NT. I think he may take it the hardest and it would probably come better from you than anyone else. He admires you so much."

"I'll make it the first stop. And I could use your support tonight when I inform the rest of the folks about the massacre at Fort Pillow."

"I'll be there." Helen recanted.

"Thank you, Helen." Man said exiting the front door and making his way towards his horse. Once more tears rolled down his ebony cheeks as he threw his leg over the saddle and turned the thoroughbred in the direction of his home. On the way back he contemplated exacting revenge on Bedford and his militia but realized the futility of even considering retaliation and had to swallow hard realizing there was little to do in the way of bringing Dante and other loved ones back.

No, he was responsible for moving his people forward with their newfound freedom. Schools needed to be built, foundations needed to be erected, doctors and lawyers needed to be taught and nurtured so as to be able to combat this enemy of the Colored man.

The time of armed encounters was quickly coming to an end and the real war had only just begun. They needed to be well armed and well equipped. And Lord knows the Colored man could hardly expect to fight an armed war with the man who makes the arms.

No, there had to be a way to combat his aggression without armed confrontation. And to his way of thinking education and civility was the way.

Tanya had done as he'd asked and thirty of her finest troops lay the way as the people came in droves despite the chilly spring air and were now assembled on the front grass when Man rode in on his pearl, gray stallion looking nothing short of the young king he now was.

One of T.'s own private guards dressed in all black gathered the horse in as Man dismounted and climbed the five steps of the front porch. At six foot six inches he stood head and shoulders above the tallest man there and had a clear vision of the crowd before him.

"Ladies and gentleman, I guess you're wondering why I've called you all here on this rather, chilly evening. And I wish I could say I have good news to share but sadly I don't.

The last time we had a gathering of such proportions was to announce that President Lincoln had signed the Emancipation Proclamation freeing each and everyone one of us. It was a glorious day, a day for celebration a day of jubilee. There however was a price to be paid for this freedom and many of our boys, our husbands our brothers and our fathers thought our freedom was worth giving their lives for. And I'm sorry to say that on this day a wire has come through stating that three hundred of our young men have given their lives for this newfound freedom."

A huge shriek went up from the crowd.

"I'm sure quite a few of you remember the Major General Nathan Bedford Forrest who tried to attack us here at Maroon a few months ago. Well, In retaliation he massacred three hundred men after they held up a white flag of surrender. Shot them down in cold blood he did." Man said pausing to let the words sink in. And again there were shrieks and cries throughout the massive crowd.

"Now I am sure that you are as I am both shocked and devastated by this tragedy and utter devastation and usually it would be up to my discretion as to the type of restraint and discretion that should be taken in lieu of this but since so many of you have been affected by this tragedy I'm asking you what course of action should be taken in this particular case.

All of you who truly believe that the Lord should be the mediator in this case let me see a show of hands." A smattering of hands went up. "To all those that think retribution should be ours let me see a show of hands." A slew of hands went up far out shadowing the first group. "Then it is agreed. We ride at first dawn. For those that want to know if they lost a loved one at the hands of Major General Nathan Forest Bedford please come forward and these ladies will check their lists." Man said making his way into his home where he sat and cried inconsolably until the wee hours of the morning.

Roman Nose was back and ready to ride when Man made his way to the stables early the next morning.

"Good to see you my old friend," Roman Nose said hugging his friend tightly. "I hear we lost one of our dearest friends and brothers."

"Yes."

"And how are you holding up my friend?"

"He was one of my oldest friends and always my protector."

"You must be deeply hurt," Roman Nose added.

"You just don't know the sadness I feel. And not only for me but for his wife and nine kids."

"I can imagine. But and not to rub salt in the wound but you should have eliminated Bedford when you had the chance. Again you let your enemy off the hook and again he comes back to haunt you. Now you seek revenge when this should have ended when you had the chance to end it. Just facts my friend."

"I'm ashamed to admit but T. told me the same thing."

"I'm ashamed to admit it but it has come back to haunt me once again. I was only trying to follow in my papa's footsteps but these people have no souls, where we matter. It almost seems as if they have no heart, no compassions towards us as a people."

"They don't. You are merely another of their beasts of burden. Here to do their heavy lifting. Your soul purpose is to make them wealthy. Other than that you serve little or no purpose. And now that you are rising to take arms against them it is tantamount to heresy in their eyes and from their point of view you and all those like you should be wiped from the earth. And Man that is what they intend to do. Can you not see that?"

"I'm afraid I'm beginning to. As sad as it seems, it's becoming painfully obvious that too many of these Crackers see me as no more than my usefulness to their quest for wealth. To far too many I'm nothing and will never be more than chattel."

"And the sooner you come to accept that the easier your life be."

"Tomorrow we leave with six hundred troops to serve Major General Forest with a little payback for his indiscretions. Can I count on you joining us my friend?"

"It is not so easy to answer that now Man. My new wife is somewhat adamant about the battles I choose and in the case of the Major General I already can tell you her response. She will say, 'now hon, you and I both know that his has become a personal vendetta between Man and the Major General because of the unfortunate loss of his boyhood friend Dante. But why should we see the loss of lives compounded because of his failure to put this man away in the first place? This will only lead to an unnecessary loss of life and a chain of events that I don't really see you having a role in. It is so futile and unnecessary and will only result in more lives being lost."

"Are these your words or hers Roman Nose?"

"They would be hers but I would have to agree with them. And yet you already know that if you were to ask me directly to go I could not refuse you my brother."

"Well, and being the fact that you are a newlywed I will not impose that on you. The Lord knows that if anything happened to you I would never be able to face Chastity again or be able to live with myself. But this I will ask of you my brother and my friend. I would ask that you and Dido would be responsible for the safety of Maroon."

"I am honored that you would entrust in me such an honor. I will guard them with my life," Roman Nose said turning and hugging his good friend Man tightly. "And as I won't see you in the morning I wish you the best of luck in your endeavors. And though I know that you feel compelled to go to avenge Dante's murder I will tell you as a friend that I don't think it is a wise move and think you're going will only compound matters."

"And I thank you for honesty, Roman Nose but you know I must go."

"I know and I will send Little Bear and some braves with you to help assure your victory my friend."

"Thank you. And I will see you upon my return." Man said hugging Roman Nose before making his leave for the night.

Chapter 26

The sun was nowhere to be found when Man walked to the stables that brisk April morning. Man along with his wife by his side mounted their stallions in their all-Black uniforms and proceeded out of the pasture in front of the all-Black brigade of military might with the wind at their backs and escorted by the courage and resolve needed to fight a superior force. No words were spoken of who should lead and who should remain home to guard the good civilians of Maroon. And despite his good reason this was a fight, a battle that could not be avoided or reckoned with. There was no place for reason or discard now. There was no place for good intentions, solemn resolve or good sense. There was only a place for retribution and retaliation.

And so before the sun had a chance to warm the world as Maroon had come to know it Man and Tanya led the way with close to seven hundred of their troops out of Kansas and into

Tennessee where scouts soon picked up on Major General Nathan

Bedford Forrest's last known whereabouts. From the last reports

the Major General and his well renowned cavalry had been

wreaking havoc throughout Alabama and Tennessee.

When he scouts picked up his latest known whereabouts he

was right outside of Memphis which was heavily fortified by

Federal troops. From all estimations his army consisted of several

cavalry regiments of no more than fifteen hundred men as opposed

to close to six thousand Union troops. Any attempt to attack the

city were seen as suicidal and yet he was on his way there with no

sight of support. Still no one put anything by Forrest, the wizard

of the saddle as he'd been come to be known. Said to be one of the

greatest strategists of the Confederacy the Federalist still opted to

look the other way upon his arrival.

"When they said an all-Black force was headed this way I

knew it was my family from Maroon," Lieutenant General

Chivington said hugging Man and Tanya as his officers stood idly by watching in shock. And then and with no further ado he approached Helen.

"Helen, it is so good to see you. I only wish it had been under different circumstances. I'm terribly sorry for your loss. I only wish I'd been there when it all went down. The news came to me as a shock as well. I can only say that his loss was as much a part of the army's fault as they are the Confederates. When you are outnumbered by as many as they were at Fort Pillow you just naturally concede. There is no valor in dying when the odds are solely in your opponents favor as they were.

Not giving any stock or relevance to Bedford's actions, surrendering was a no-brainer and was the only course of action. But in assuring his own escape the officer in charge chose not to surrender.

Being the soldier that Dante was he saw the situation as futile and tried to surrender and Bedford's men under his directions shot them all down in cold-blood.

Again I can't profess to tell you how badly I feel about this whole ordeal. I am truly sorry for our loss. I have never had a soldier serve with me that I had as much respect for as I did for your husband. He not only was a fine soldier but even more than that he was a fine man. I am proud to say that he was most of all my friend."

"Thank you general but as I told Man there's hardly anything for you to be sorry for. D knew the hazards that soldiering entailed and if anything he was a soldier and embraced it, including the hazards. He would have given anything to stay in and be the best at it. And he was. And though I am grateful for your condolences those are not our concerns now. We are here to relieve all the wives and children who have also lost loved ones at

370

the hands of Major General Bedford Forrest. If he'd beaten them in a battle it would have been one thing and we would have accepted it though begrudgingly. It was the fact that we released him and his men and this is how he chose to repay us; by shooting down our men, who chose to surrender at point blank range and in cold blood. That is what we are having trouble swallowing."

"And I completely understand. Well, we're still trying to see what he's up to. We have Memphis fortified with close to six thousand men and he arrives with only fifteen hundred men and no other supporting forces--and well—and though it appears suspicious I would be the last to undermine Bedford. He is both shrewd and cunning and has exacted some devastating losses on us in the past three or four months."

"Well, general I can assure you that Maroon will not be outfoxed by him again," Tanya added.

371

"What I would like to do first general is to meet him and sit down and parley with him," Man suggested.

"Are you sure you want to meet with him Man? I don't think you'll have the same sway as you had with me."

Tanya laughed.

"General, as close as you and Man have become I don't think you really understand my husband. Thomas has an inquisitive mind and at this point I hardly thinks he wants to get to know the man to see where his weaknesses are or how he can out maneuver him on the battlefield. I think Thomas simply wants to know at this juncture what kind of man could slaughter three hundred soldiers and not bat an eye. I just think he wants to know what type of God if any lives within the heart and soul of a man such as this." Tanya said cordially.

"Well, if that's the case then I will send forth a messenger to see if he'll meet with you. But don't be surprised if he turns you down. He's a diehard Confederate and a racist to boot."

"Of that I am sure. But nothing fails but a try," Man said the sadness obvious in his voice.

"Corporal."

"Yes, general," the young man said.

"Take this massage and give it to Major General Bedford with the quickness."

"Yes sir," the young man said taking the handwritten note and jumping upon his horse.

"In the meantime, let me get you something to eat and have you reacquainted with what's left of your family and friends," Chivington said hugging Thomas again. "It really is so good to see you all again. Those day of fishing for catfish seem so long ago but still remain as some of my fondness memories of being out west. You don't know how I long for those days."

"Believe me general, he misses Man misses them too," Tanya added.

Chapter 27

An hour or so later the young cavalry man returned with a message saying that Major William Bedford Forrest would gladly and humbly meet with the Maroon contingent in the Gayoso House Hotel in downtown Memphis on Beale Street.

Forty five minutes before their meeting Chivington sent troops in to canvas the area and make sure Forrest had no troops stationed to ambush the party and after the troops reported back and said they found nothing to believe there was any kind of plot behind the meeting Helen, Tanya and Man rode in accompanied by a small group of Tanya's elite troops.

The luxurious Gayoso Hotel had long ago been evacuated but was still exquisite and pristine in appearance.

"Shots anyone?" Helen said as she poured herself three fingers of an exquisite brandy.

"Pour me one too," Tanya said grinning. "The road can make you acquire quite a thirst. Man?"

"No, I'm good and I'm gonna need you ladies to be on your toes too. Why don't you take the bottle and hold it until after the meeting. I don't want anything to go awry."

"Awry? Hell, what's to go wrong other than I shoot this bastard and who would have qualms with that? Hell, the Feds have been trying to get rid of this Cracker since the beginning of the war. I'd only be doing them a favor. Lest you forget this is the man who killed my husband and the father of my eight orphaned children. And the Bible plainly states plainly 'an eye for an eye'," Helen said breathing deeply. It was clear to all that the brandy was already taking hold and Man viewed the worse.

"Remember Helen that we are better than these people. It will do you know justice to kill this man although he needs to be dead. He took my brother and best friend but what he did was not right and for you to kill him in cold blood under a flag of truce would be no better than what he did.

We as Black folk must appeal to our God and to our better nature in circumstances such as these where murder comes easily. We cannot stoop as low as our enemy and then ask God to accept us and to bless us when we are in direct opposition to Him."

"Shut the hell up Man. I'm tired of all your righteous talk about God and upholding all that's right. I'm in pain now and God can't fix that. We can't all be saints," she shouted.

"No, we can't but our job is to try. We must try and aspire to be Godlike. Now give me your word you will not do anything other than talk."

There was a long period with Helen lifting the bottle of brandy up to her mouth and taking long swallows before turning to her girls and telling them to find an empty wagon and load it with cases of liquor from the bar.

"That's not the answer to D's death Helen and I need an answer from you before the general gets here." Man said approaching the bar where Helen was standing. Throwing down the last shot she turned to him, swayed a bit and then looking straight at him said.

"Damn you Man. You know as well as I do that this son-of-a-bitch should be dead but you're right," she said pausing to weigh her thoughts. "Okay Man, he gets a pass this time but he's mine the next time we meet in battle," she said before sliding both handgun and rifle towards Man.

"He's yours only if I don't get to him first," Man said before taking her in his arms. Together they both wept openly.

It was at this time that the door of the hotel swung open. A tall, stately man, of no more than six feet, neatly shaven and manicured with a receding hairline and deep penetrating eyes strode in.

"Nathan Bedford Forrest at your service," he said with a warm smile that flooded the room. "I was told that you ladies and gentlemen summoned me to take part in a little parley."

"Name's Tanya. Tanya Mann and this is my husband Thomas Man. Most people just call him Man general."

"Please. General is just a title and among friends who needs titles?" he said smiling congenially. "I was told you wanted to speak to me and that some of you have friends and family that lost their lives at Fort Pillow. If that's the case then I am glad that I was summoned today. I would very much like to clear that up.

As you know we are in the midst of a very heated debate over states' rights. Some would like to call it a war over slavery. I do not believe that's the true cause of the war and would hate to believe that the case. In any case, I fight to preserve state's rights and I'm sure you all know war means fighting and fighting means killing. I would like to think that I am a Christian man and as you all know Christ had his wars. And even though our Christ came out on the wrong end of the battle there was killing."

"Please stop there general. We are all aware of what war is. We as Black folk have been fighting all our lives. We have been fighting and killing all of our lives just to assure our freedom and liberty: something that folks such as yourselves take for granted. I believe you call it an inalienable right.

The difference between you and I is we did not go looking for a war. It was bestowed on us as was sin by Adam and Eve. Our Blackness is tantamount to the original sin. We did nothing to ask for it. It was not debatable as is your so-called war over states' rights but it was our birthright. And even though it was we sought to show compassion and mercy as our Lord has shown us. Yet, we are having difficulty understanding why you do not show the same compassion towards us. When we had you outnumbered and

outgunned in Kansas we had the grace and mercy to let you go
free.

That's why I called this meeting. I wanted to meet the man
who can show retribution by killing the same man that let you live.
Where is the compassion there?" Man said staring the general right
in his eyes.

"You make many a fine point my friend but again this is
war and I can make no apologies once the bugle sounds. But I will
say this in my defense. If you surrender, you shall be treated as
prisoners of war, but if I have to storm your works, you may
expect no quarter.

In the case of Fort Pillow I asked the commander in charge
who was clearly at a disadvantage to surrender. He chose not to.
And I am sorry if you lost friends and family members but again I
must say that war is war and war means killing. And if there are

no further questions I have a war to contend with," Bedford said standing and extending his hand.

"I am sorry but I cannot shake the hand of an enemy of the Negro," Man said standing but not extending his hand.

We have but one flag, one country; let us stand together. We may differ in color, but not in sentiment."

"I would have to beg to disagree," Man said.

"Then it is with Godspeed that I leave you all," he said on his way out the door.

By this time, Helen was fit to be tied and headed out after him.

"I'll kill the bastard. He doesn't even pretend to show any remorse and my children are fatherless."

It took Man and the ladies all they could do to restrain her. On the way back Helen cursed the Confederates, Nathan Bedford and all that had anything to do with the war. Once they'd returned and shared everything there was to share they set about plotting on how to subdue Bedford and his cavalry. As they sat there in the command post devising a strategy to end Bedford's campaign shots could be heard ringing out in the distant.

"It couldn't be Bedford. He'd be a fool to attack us with such a paltry amount of troops," Chivington mused before turning back and scouring over the plans for subduing Bedford's cavalry. It was then that the corporal who'd been sent to set up the meeting stormed in.

"General sir, Bedford's men have just stormed the Gayoso House Hotel seeking to kidnap the general's you had moved last night. They also attacked Irving Block Prison and freed almost five hundred Confederate soldiers. He may very well be planning on trying to take Memphis now."

"Even with those men he is still out manned and outgunned and he has no artillery support," Chivington responded. "He'd be a fool to try that."

"Are you ready to lead the attack now?" Tanya asked Chivington.

"No ma'am. There is no hurry. We still hold a distinct advantage. Bedford's moves are of a desperate man. We have things fully in control. Let's get a good night's sleep and give the whole thing some more thought in the morning. Our hastiness can very well result in an unnecessary loss of lives."

In the morning when they awoke they found Bedford and his army gone. And with Sherman's march through the South the Confederacy was now forced to concede defeat. Two weeks later on April 26th Robert E. Lee surrendered to Ulysses S. Grant.

Tanya read the quote from Nathan Bedford Forrest after the defeat in the local tabloids. "Obey the laws, preserve your honor, and the government to which you have surrendered can afford to be and will be magnanimous. This was Nathan Bedford Forrest's, farewell address to his men, made in Gainesville, on May 9, 1865. But this was not the last we heard of Major General Nathan Bedford Forrest and although Helen and Tanya were still adamant about chasing this man down and eliminating him permanently for his actions at Fort Pillow. Man had the effect of being one of the few people who had the unusual ability to temper her passion and intensity in times like these.

"I can think of so many other things we can do instead at times like these," he said grinning and winking at her at the same time.

"I'm really starting to think that you don't have anything else on your mind these days."

"You may be right but it's your fault. I do believe that you grow lovelier by the day my love or maybe I'm just growing

fonder of you the more I see you. I'm really not sure but one thing
I do know is that I would like nothing more than to snuggle under
that warm comforter with you and attempt to make papa happy
with some little ones," Man said grinning like a Cheshire cat.

With the war now over there seemed more hope now for
the Colored population of Maroon than ever. Man and Roman
Nose were now deeply immersed and conducting a thriving
business in appaloosas and word spread quickly and they received
much acclaim for the quality and fine breeding of their stallions.
Many said they had the finest thoroughbreds west of the
Mississippi and the horses alone made Maroon a profitable
community. Folks came from miles around seeking the valued
horses and after only a couple of years the herd had grown to more
than five thousand. And with Tanya's ingenuity Maroon not only
supplied the Army with horses but also with other supplies needed
west of the Mississippi.

Furniture and agricultural items were now marketed throughout the southwest while Dido lobbied his Washington associates to make Maroon an official stop on the Union pacific Railroad. And once word got out to Coloreds leaving the South in hordes that there was a Colored town west of the Mississippi run by Coloreds and thriving there was steady stream of new inhabitants looking to better themselves.

CPSIA information can be obtained
at www.ICGtesting.com
Printed in the USA
LVHW092255170321
681694LV00013B/1028